THE SCHOOLMARM'S CONVENIENT MARRIAGE
Frontier Matches Book 4
Published by Edwards and Williams
Copyright © 2023 by Regina Lundgren

This is a work of fiction. Names, characters, places and incidents are either the product of the author's imagination or are used fictitiously, and any resemblance to actual persons, living or dead, business establishments, events or locales is entirely coincidental.

Printed in the USA.

Cover Design and Interior Format

THE SCHOOLMARM'S CONVENIENT MARRIAGE

REGINA SCOTT

To all the schoolteachers who have instructed and inspired me over the years, especially my mother, and to the Lord, who patiently teaches us in all His ways.

CHAPTER ONE

Seattle, Washington Territory
October 1876

MUST A LADY travel to the ends of the earth to gain command of her own future?

Apparently so, for Alice Dennison could only shake her head at the telegram gripped in her gloved hand.

"I hope it isn't bad news," her friend, Ciara Weatherly, said as they stood outside the telegraph office along the wharves. The shouts of the sailors offloading goods punctuated the whir of machinery at the nearby sawmill. Tar and cedar and brine mixed for a potent aroma under skies that hovered lower and darker every moment. Or maybe it was the words she'd read that had lowered her spirits.

THIS IS UNNECESSARY RETURN AT ONCE

"Nothing that requires a reply," Alice said. "I'm sorry we delayed our visit to check."

"We always check when we come in for the mail." The voice rumbled from behind her, and she forced herself not to stiffen. Mr. Willets, who had accompanied them to town, was a giant of a fellow, towering over everyone except Mr. Drew Wallin, who was apparently a legend in the territory. Mr. Willets was also a man of few words. She had yet to determine whether it was because he had an economy of speech or because he simply knew few words.

"Then we have done our duty," she said. As they started forward, she crumpled the note and shoved it into her reticule to be summarily burned in the fire when they reached Wallin Landing.

That is, if she could remember how to rekindle the fire.

They had all been so patient with her, from Mrs. Rina Wallin, who was the lead teacher at the Lake Union School, to Alice's darling students ranging in age from five to eight. Mrs. Rina had explained the expectations of Alice's position. She had shown Alice how to clean and trim the lamps that lit her side of the two-room schoolhouse at the back of the village nestled along the shores of the lake.

And Mrs. Rina or one of the local gentlemen had repeatedly shown Alice how to lay the wood they brought her into the grate to keep the school warm as the autumn weather grew more brisk. She was the one who couldn't seem to get the wretched fire to stay lit!

She should have expected it would be a challenge to find her footing so far away from everything she'd once known, from everyone with whom she'd once thought to share her life. But she was more than ready to meet that challenge. Wallin Landing was her home now. She would do her best to be a good citizen, a good teacher, and a good friend. No more would she allow others to direct the course of her life, even if that meant remaining a spinster to the end of her days.

Ciara craned her neck to see into the bed of the wagon that had brought them to town, the breeze catching at her bonnet. Like Alice, she had dark hair, but hers seemed more easily tamed. Alice hadn't the time to pamper her hair here. So, she pulled it up and let it tumble down her back. So far, no one had protested.

"At least the things you ordered for the school came in," Ciara said. "Six slates and enough chalk to color Mount Rainier like a rainbow."

Alice's cheeks warmed, and again she chided herself. It was her classroom and her choice of instruction. She did not have to ask anyone's approval.

For once.

"The children and I like to draw pictures," she explained. "I find it helps the learning process if they can visualize what we're discussing."

"I wish you'd been around when I was in school," Ciara said with a smile. She relaxed back beside her, chocolate-colored eyes brightening. "Now, to Kellogg's for *my* supplies."

Ciara was the proprietress of the Wooden Rose Inn, the first such establishment in the settlement. And it was flourishing thanks to her expertise in cooking, another skill Alice lacked. But then, she hadn't been raised to cook and clean, merely manage those who did.

"Best we move fast," Mr. Willets said with a look to the sky.

Likely he was right. In Cawthorn, where she'd been raised, and in Boston, where she'd attended a teachers' college for the last year, rains often came in the evenings with a sudden passion, then faded to leave everything fresh and clean. Here, rain spit and spat in fussy little mists, often for days at a time, before the sun came out as if opening its arms for an embrace. But the sky had been stingy today, threatening to pour but never letting go of a single drop.

"Then let's stop by the Pastry Emporium first," Ciara said. "I want Alice to meet my sister."

Frisco and Sutter, twin boys who were in Mrs. Rina's class, had made sure to tell Alice all about Ciara's famous older sister. Maddie O'Rourke Haggerty had opened the first and now the premiere bakery in Seattle.

"Everyone loves her cinnamon buns best," Sutter had said with a reverent lift of his blond brows.

"Her gingersnaps," his brother had insisted.

Sutter had shoved him in the chest. "Cinnamon buns."

"Gingersnaps!"

"Perhaps I'll see if I can bring back some of both," Alice had said, "for those who remember their manners."

They had instantly stood upright like tin soldiers and vowed to be complete gentlemen in her absence.

Now, Mr. Willets set his hands on Ciara's waist and boosted her onto the wagon's bench. Alice waited patiently for her turn. But the big logger seemed suddenly at odds. He shifted on his feet, and his gaze, a lighter gray than the sky, darted here and there like that of one of her students caught in an infraction.

"Is there a problem, Mr. Willets?" she asked, frowning.

"No." She could see his Adam's apple bob as he swallowed. Unlike many of the men in the area, he was clean shaven, the planes of his face firm and rather pleasant to look upon. His hair reminded her of a fading fire, russet and warm. And his physique in the flannel collarless shirt and wool trousers could only be called impressive.

Not that a lady should notice such things.

Alice lifted her arms a little to encourage him. "I'm afraid I cannot climb up on my own, sir. Would you mind?"

He sighed as if she'd asked him to perform the labors of Hercules, then put his hands on her waist. His fingers spanned the width, and suddenly she found it difficult to breathe even though his touch was light. Then, *whoosh!* He all but tossed her up onto the bench as if she had burned him. She clutched at Ciara to keep from falling into her friend's lap.

"Are you in such a hurry, Jesse?" Ciara asked with a frown as she helped Alice settle herself.

The third overskirt on her gown snagged on a splinter of wood, and she had to tug the blue-sprigged material free. She'd thought she'd chosen such practical gowns when she'd sent her trunk ahead and stolen away in the middle of the night to catch the train west, but the silks and linens of summer had proven impractical here. Her next pay would go toward something more useful. Wool. No overskirts. No lace.

This time she was the one who sighed.

But she kept a smile on her face as Mr. Willets climbed into place beside them and drove them up the hill to Second Avenue, where Mrs. Haggerty had her bakery.

"I see a crowd has already gathered," she told Ciara as the wagon drew next to the boardwalk. "Testimony to your sister's skills, no doubt."

But Ciara wasn't smiling, and Alice realized why. No lights gleamed inside the bakery. Someone had affixed a large sign, hastily scrawled by the look of the lettering, on the big front window, proclaiming the establishment closed. Several men were clustered around, muttering.

"Maddie never closes except on Sundays," Ciara said, voice trembling. "Even when she came out for my wedding, she baked ahead and had someone keep the shop open. Take me to Fourth Avenue, Jesse. I need to see my family."

Jesse nodded. Family came first. He'd heard his father say that many a time, and he believed it, even if he'd chosen a different path than his brothers. He urged the horses around the corner and up the steep hill for Fourth, where many of the nicer houses had been built.

Ciara pointed out which one belonged to her sister, but he thought he might have guessed. Like many of the sweets Maddie Haggerty baked, the top dripped with curlicues that looked like icing.

"Stay here," Ciara said as he reined in the horses,

"until I know who's sick and with what. That's the only explanation for Maddie missing a day of work." She clambered over Miss Dennison and scrambled down before Jesse could come around to help her.

Leaving him sitting with the schoolmarm.

He stayed on his side of the bench.

She stayed on hers.

"I do hope no one is terribly ill," she murmured in a voice that the songbirds must envy. That was the thing with Miss Dennison. Everything about her was dainty and sweet, from the shiny black hair that tumbled down behind her back like an obsidian waterfall to her delicately featured face and the slender figure her fancy clothes outlined. Even her hands fluttered like little birds. Next to her, Jesse felt like a giant.

A great, lumbering, not-too-bright giant.

"Probably just took a chill," he managed.

Immediately she turned her gaze to his. She had eyes the purple-blue of the wildflowers his sisters like to pick, and they too often brimmed with tears that could make a man promise anything to see her smile again.

"Do you think so?" she breathed.

"Sure," he said. He caught his balance and realized he'd slid as far as dignity allowed to his side of the bench.

"Have you a great deal of experience with such things?" she asked, and there was no skepticism in her tone, only a wide-eyed wonder. "Some training as a physician?"

"No," Jesse said. "Only nine little brothers and sisters."

Now her lashes were fluttering too. "Nine!"

Did she think that a good thing? A bad thing? He'd met folks in both camps. Not that it mattered. He wouldn't have traded any of his brothers or sisters, for all each of them had given him a bad time or two along the way. In fact, he'd once dared to hope he might have a passel of little ones of his own. That hope dimmed with each passing year. Too few women, too many expectations.

Her delicate black brows drew together, and so did his stomach. "I don't believe I've met any of them," she said. "Do they attend the school?"

"My family lives near Puget City, closer to Olympia." There. A full sentence with subject and verb. Ma would be so proud. He could hear her in his head.

You're a fine man, Jesse. You're kind and sensible, and you don't use that height and strength of yours to bully. You have no reason to be bashful.

"Olympia," she said, brow clearing. "Yes, the town at the southern end of Puget Sound. It is the territorial capital and the third city incorporated in the territory."

She sounded as if she were reciting from memory. He knew the same facts, but his family's ranch meant far more to him. When he thought of home, he felt the wind rippling the grasses, caught the flash of a salmon leaping out of the Nisqually. He heard his brothers and sisters laughing as they hunted the woods for blackcaps and mushrooms. He caught the scent of milk in the pail, of bread baking and steak sizzling. So, he just nodded.

"I would very much like to see Olympia someday," she said. "Perhaps you'd care to share your experiences there."

The memories evaporated from his mind, leaving nothing but a wall of white broader than Rainier's glaciers. That had ever been his problem. He had seldom been the center of attention in his family. He didn't know how to deal with it when strangers focused on him. Would he sound as if he were bragging? Would he sound illiterate?

He was just thankful to see Ciara returning, hands fisted in her skirts.

Until she spoke.

"Leave," she said, voice once more trembling. "Go back to the Landing. Tell Kit I'll be home when I can."

"Oh, Ciara!" Miss Dennison cried, reaching out a hand toward her. "What is it?"

"They're not sure," Ciara admitted with a glance back

to the house, "and I haven't been inside yet, so you are both safe. My brother-in-law Michael spoke to me through the glass on the front window. Maddie's sick, and he fears it's smallpox."

Jesse's grip on the reins tightened, and Lancelot, the lead horse, protested. He forced his hands to relax even as his mind whirled. He'd never lived through a smallpox epidemic, but his parents told stories of the fast-moving disease. Its rash could disfigure, even kill! Was Ciara's family safe? Was his?

Miss Dennison must have heard of the disease as well, for she clutched the sideboard, and he could only hope she wouldn't faint.

"Oh, no!" she cried. "I heard rumors in San Francisco when I came through but I didn't think the disease had progressed beyond the city."

"We don't know yet," Ciara cautioned. "But I can't leave them. And I don't dare bring it home to baby Grace. Tell Kit I love him."

Now her body was trembling. So was Miss Dennison's. Jesse raised his head. He was strong, he was healthy. It was his duty to help others who might be affected.

"We will," Miss Dennison promised. "Please, be careful."

Ciara nodded. And all Jesse could do was urge the horses forward again.

"How horrid," Miss Dennison said, voice small and frightened as they headed for the road out to Wallin Landing. "Of course we must carry her words to her dear husband and baby. I will pray for her safety and the health of her sister and her family."

Jesse nodded. He'd pray too. Not out loud with a lot of words. God didn't expect that, and he was forever grateful for the fact.

Seattle was always pushing outward, but the wagon soon reached the brush that marked the edge. The schoolmarm fell silent as they entered the tunnel of trees that covered the road out to the Landing. It was cooler here, but it wasn't just the overlapping branches of fir and cedar. The temperature was dropping. A storm was coming. He just had to get them to the Landing before it hit.

He slapped down the reins. "Lancelot! Percival! Yah!"

"Lancelot and Percival?" she asked, voice sounding brittle, as if she was searching for anything to talk about besides the danger they were fleeing.

"The horses," he clarified.

"Named for the knights of King Arthur's court? How marvelous! Are they yours, Mr. Willets?"

She *was* new. "Mr. Wallin's. He allows the use of them."

"Which Mr. Wallin?" she asked. He was relieved when she continued speaking as if answering her own question. "Not Mr. Drew—he is your employer. I believe Mr. Simon has horses, but they would be needed at the farm, so I doubt he could allow others to use them on a regular basis. Mr. James, the proprietor of the mercantile, perhaps?"

Jesse grinned at her. "That's right."

She stared at him, and his smile faded. What had he done wrong now?

She dropped her gaze, fiddled with the little beaded sack in her lap. A shiver went through her.

Well, of course, Jesse. If you noticed the cold in your flannels, how do you think she feels in that frilly dress?

"Extra blanket in the bed," he offered.

She twisted to pull up the thick wool he had packed before they'd headed out that morning. "How very wise of you to think to bring this."

Once again, she was making him feel clever. But the weather mocked him, daring him to try to make the run. The trees were starting to talk, swaying and gossiping in breathy rustles as the wind freshened. In the distance, he thought he heard a rumble.

Lancelot and Percival picked up their paces, as if they had heard it too and longed for the safety of their barn.

"I suppose some would say we should have stayed in town," she ventured, wrapping the blanket around her shoulders. "With the weather and the lack of a chaperone. But we are out of doors and in easy view of anyone along the road."

The West Lake Road had become more widely traveled over the years as folks filed claims along the hillside above David Denny's. But anyone with any sense would be heading for home this afternoon.

The trees began to whip in earnest, and the first lightning bolt flashed across the sky above their tops. She cried out and hunched closer to him. Lancelot tossed his head at the noise.

Best thing Jesse could do for them all was keep calm.

"Rain's coming," he said. "Put that blanket up over your head."

She started to do as he'd bid, but she unfolded the blanket further, then flipped it up over his head too. He smiled at her thoughtfulness.

Ahead, with a mighty creak of protest, one of the firs toppled.

Lancelot reared in his traces, and Jesse clung to the reins, fighting for control. Thunder roared, shaking the wagon. Both horses shuddered. And then the rain started, sluicing out of the clouds.

Miss Dennison didn't scream. She didn't tremble. She just looked at him with her great purple-blue eyes brimming and said, "Please, Mr. Willets, won't you save us?"

Jesse raised his head, pulling the blanket partially off her ebony hair. "Yes, ma'am. You can count on me."

CHAPTER TWO

PERHAPS SHE SHOULDN'T believe him. Alice didn't know him, and she'd been highly disappointed by those who had been closest to her. Still, much as she'd vowed to be in command of her future, she was out of her depths at the moment. She couldn't drive a team of horses under the best of conditions, much less in a storm.

And he had an air about him. The confident tilt of his chin, the certainty in his gray eyes, and the breadth of his shoulders said this man could do what he claimed. And he did have the nicest smile. She'd forgotten what she was about to say when she'd spied it a few moments ago.

The wind blew the blanket up behind her, and rain splattered her back, chilling her shoulders above her stays. She gasped.

He jumped down and reached for her. "Let's get you settled, then I can help the horses."

Alice shook herself. He was right. They needed to move. Lancelot and Percival—what marvelous names!—were fretting, their powerful bodies shifting and the shaft connecting them to the wagon creaking. She let Mr. Willets hand her down onto the side of the road.

He nodded to a cedar some five feet away. It was nearly as wide as the schoolhouse. "Put your back to that. I'll join you in a minute."

One hand clutching the blanket, the other clutching her skirts, the ribbons of her reticule wrapped about her wrist, she picked her way through the thrashing ferns to the needle-littered carpet under the cedar. The dry, musty scent brushed her nose, as if she'd opened a chest filled with the comforts of home.

The rain had yet to penetrate the branches, so she pulled the blanket from her head. By the time she focused on the road again, Mr. Willets was leading the horses closer as well. They dragged the wagon over the brush, flattening it further. Coaxing and calling, he convinced them to stop so that the wagon sat across the tree lengthwise. Then he began working to unhitch the pair, fingers slipping on the wet chains.

She tried to think of some way to help, but she knew even less about unhitching horses than she did about tending fires, so she could only stay out of his way. Somehow he managed to free the horses from the traces and tied them to the closest low, large branch, where they could stand or lie comfortably. The massive bodies shifted, eyes showing white, as the thunder boomed again. She knew the feeling.

Throwing the blanket back over her head, she ventured out into the rain to lay a hand on the closest.

"It's all right," she murmured to the pair, whose heads bobbed up and down as if seeking to make her acquaintance. "The storm will pass soon."

But it didn't. In fact, it seemed to be building itself into something rather fierce. The brush whipped about as if it would yank itself from its roots. The trees moaned and cracked. She could not see their tops, but more than one came down with a rattle and a roar, causing the horses to jerk and neigh. Worse was the roll of thunder that didn't seem to end.

Mr. Willets didn't seem disturbed by it all. He made

noises to the horses that quieted them and oddly soothed her as well. If he wasn't worried about this havoc, perhaps it wasn't as bad as she thought.

He nodded to her. "Move aside."

"Move aside?" Alice asked, confused, but her words bounced off his back as he started around the wagon. "Why?"

He reached the far side. Perhaps he wanted to save her supplies. Surely the chalk would melt in this downpour! Instead, he braced each hand against a side support and leaned in.

The wagon inched closer to the tree, out of the rain. Alice blinked, then scrambled out of its path.

Muscles bunched under the soaked flannel shirt that clung to his body as he shoved again. The wheels dug into the soft dirt, but the other side of the wagon bumped the cedar.

Alice stared.

He straightened and nodded as if satisfied. "Under you go."

She could only do as he'd asked, her skirts puddling about her as she sank onto the ground and crawled under his makeshift roof.

A moment more, and he crawled under with her, shoving the chalk and slates before him.

"There," he said, lower lip out, as he managed to fold his large frame into their shelter. "That should do it."

"Mr. Willets," she said. "You astonish me."

The light was fading, from the storm, the wagon's cover, and the impending night, but she thought his cheeks were pinking. "Just practical," he said. "There won't be room for the horses, but they wouldn't like it much anyway. Horses prefer to see what's coming."

She had learned the value of that as well, but she had to admit his little nest was cozy. What rain fell from the cedar pooled in the wagon's bed, keeping them dry. Well, mostly dry. She eyed his wet clothing as he settled on the ground next to her.

"You must take this," she said, unpeeling the blanket. "It's not entirely dry, but it should help. We wouldn't want you to take a chill."

He stretched his long legs as far as their shelter allowed. "You likely need it more than me."

"Nonsense. You bore the brunt of the weather." When he made no move to take the material from her, Alice pulled it back. He was probably being gallant, but she'd had more than one fellow on her way West try trickery to get her closer. *Sit next to me, Miss Dennison. I'll keep you warm.* Still, she would never forgive herself if he sickened because of his kindness.

"I insist," she said, wiggling closer to him. "We can share it."

He cast her a glance that seemed equal parts surprise and suspicion. Goodness! She might think *she* was the one attempting a seduction!

"It is only practical, as you said," she told him primly.

Reluctance showing in each slow movement, he accepted a corner and draped it over his back.

"Sorry we can't light a fire," he said, voice nearly as deep as the thunder. "Wouldn't be safe."

She could see that. "I think what you did was inspired. We should be able to stay here until this storm blows itself out, then continue on our way."

He shook his head. "It's not blowing out before dark. We're stuck here until morning."

About to settle beside him, Alice stiffened. "Morning! We cannot spend the night together."

Even as she said it, she knew she was doomed. He was becoming a shadow in the growing darkness. If the storm ended right now, he would never be able to see the road to guide the horses, much less get them past that tree that had fallen. Who knew how many more had blocked the road? They couldn't go back to Seattle, not with smallpox threatening. And if they somehow managed to pick their way along without wagon or horse, they would be at the mercy of those creatures who prowled the darkness—lynx, mountain lion, bear, wolf.

"Oh, dear." She sank back onto the ground. "We truly are in trouble."

As if to prove as much, another tree came thundering down to the north of them.

Fear broke free, dousing her in cold worse than the rain. She pressed her hands to her face and smothered a sob.

Strong arms came around her, held her gently. "We'll be all right," he murmured. "I won't let anything happen to you."

She had believed his promise before, but doubts crept in with the dark.

The storm finally fretted away to nothing, and the horses at last consented to lie down next to the wagon. Jesse reckoned it was around midnight. Miss Dennison had shared the blanket with him, but it was her slender body that kept him warm. That, and the way her head had dropped against his shoulder as she'd fallen asleep. He'd put one arm around her to keep her from tumbling further. Still, a fellow could take pride in knowing he'd had a hand in enabling those even breaths as she slept.

He couldn't help wondering, though. Why had Miss Dennison come all the way to Wallin Landing from somewhere near Boston? She was clever, sweet-natured, and awfully pretty. She might have had her pick of fellows to marry. That's what most gals did—find a fellow they admired who admired them back and got married. Even the Mercer Belles, whose number included Ciara's sister and several of the Wallin wives, had mostly married, though many had originally come seeking work rather than husbands.

Of course, when Asa Mercer had brought them from back East, the War Between the States had just ended, leaving few eligible men behind. Surely that wouldn't be the case now, more than ten years later. And there had to be places between here and Boston that needed her skills. So what had driven the little schoolmarm clean across the country?

He must have fallen asleep still thinking, because the next thing he knew, a jay was squawking. He opened his eyes to find Miss Dennison gazing up at him. He hastily removed his arm, wincing as he realized it had fallen asleep too.

"Is it morning?" she asked.

Enough light trickled under the wagon that he could answer her with surety. "Yes." He pulled off the blanket, tucked it to his chest, and crawled out from under the wagon.

A weak sun struggled past branches hanging wet and forlorn. The spiky fronds of fern and lacy leaves of huckleberry had been nearly flattened. More than one tree lay collapsed, branches reaching for the sky as if begging for help. Moisture hung heavy in the air.

Lancelot surged to his feet, whickering a greeting, and Jesse rubbed a hand down the long, black nose. "Sorry I couldn't fit you under the wagon too."

Percival, who had also risen, nodded as if accepting his apology. He gave that horse a pat as well before using the blanket to rub them down. The cedar had protected them from most of the rain, thank the good Lord, but he checked them over nonetheless.

A rustle behind him told him Miss Dennison was trying to shimmy out. He turned and took her hand, lifting her gently into the light. Her black hair was a tangled mass down her back, and her frilly skirts were filmed with dirt and speckled with cedar needles. At least the storm had kept even the predators in their dens.

She looked around them. "Oh, my." Once more she turned those big eyes on him, and he couldn't look away. "Whatever shall we do, Mr. Willets?"

He shook himself and tossed the blanket into the wagon. "Can't drive. Too many trees down. Best we start walking."

She leaned forward and twisted her head to look toward the horses, sending fresh curls bouncing, black as jet. "Couldn't we ride?"

He gave Percival another pat. "No."

She faced him, and her lips tightened a moment before she spoke again. "I require additional explanation, sir."

He kept forgetting she hadn't been in the area long. She didn't seem to know much about horses either, or she might have realized the problem.

"We don't have saddles," he pointed out. "I could go bareback, but you can't in those skirts. I could put you up in front of me sidesaddle-like, but making a horse carry two would be hard on him for the distance we have to travel. Mr. James is mighty particular about the care of his horses."

"Oh." She slumped as if defeated.

"We'll take it slow," he promised, moving to untie the team. "I'll hold the horses. You can hold your chalk."

"The chalk?" Once more her lashes fluttered before her gaze flashed back to his face. "Of course, the chalk. The slates could wait to be retrieved. The chalk would melt if left among the elements too long. How very sensible of you, Mr. Willets."

He was beginning to wonder why she continued to be amazed when he said or did anything that made sense. But then, she wouldn't be the first to assume his size and silence meant he wasn't very smart.

He led Lancelot and Percival through the forest to the

road as best he could, detouring them around the big fir that had fallen last night. The road ahead was littered with debris, but nothing they couldn't pick their way through or around. Glancing back, he found that she had emerged from the forest as well, turning the blanket into a sling around one shoulder. Cradled in the center was the box of chalk.

She held up her hands. "I thought it might be wise to have my hands free, so I can help you if needed."

Jesse grinned. "Smart. Why don't you pick us some huckleberries for breakfast?"

She frowned at the bushes. "Huckleberries?"

Jesse nodded to the cluster of bushes just off the road, their leaves a brighter green than the fir needles. "Might be a few left this late in the season."

She cast him a look filled with doubt, but she minced over to the bushes. Jesse let the horses graze on a patch of nettles while she picked through the bushes. A few moments later, she returned to his side, hands cupped around her treasure.

"Mighty nice of you," he said, picking up a couple of the tiny red berries.

"It's not much," she admitted. "But it's something. Thank you for pointing them out. I'm still learning the native plants and animals."

The last word seemed to have reminded her of their situation, for she studied the forest as if expecting a bear to lumber out.

"Not too many plants left to harvest this time of year," he said, tugging on the lines to get the horses moving again. "And most of the bigger critters were scared off ages ago."

She frowned as she followed him, keeping the remaining berries in one hand so she could eat them with the other, her little beaded sack dangling from one wrist. "I was certain Ciara mentioned a lynx in the area recently."

"There was that. Gone now."

"You're certain?" she pressed.

"Can't be certain about what any animal is going to do," he said with a shrug. "But Mr. John and Kit tracked it and scared it good. I doubt it'll be back."

She drew in a deep breath as if he'd allayed her concerns. Then she brightened. "Is that the lake?"

He saw it too, glimmering cold and gray through the trees. "Yes."

"How close are we to Wallin Landing?"

"Another half an hour, give or take."

She sighed.

They trudged along, Jesse pausing every so often when he spotted something the horses or he and Miss Dennison could eat. She was more durable than he'd expected. She never complained or fussed. But she did seem to have a lot of questions.

"Were you born in Olympia?" she asked as he stopped to drag a larger limb out of the way.

"No," he said, shoving the branch into the forest. "Virginia."

"Virginia?" she asked, watching him. "What brought you so far West?"

He wanted to ask the same of her, but he urged the horses forward again instead. "My father brought us to California for the Gold Rush."

"And did he find his pot of gold?" she asked.

He could hear the snap of her skirts as she tried to keep up with him and slowed his pace. "No. He decided the area wasn't a safe place for a growing family. So he kept moving us north, until we finally settled near Puget City above the Nisqually delta."

"I don't recall hearing of a gold strike there," she mused. "Is there another sort of mine your father works at now?"

He wasn't sure why she cared. "He isn't a miner. He keeps cows."

She scrunched up her face. "Cows?"

She had to have heard of a cow. Even if she had been raised in a big city like Boston, there was one in the field near the school now, the Wallins having given a milk cow to Ciara and Kit Weatherly on their marriage.

"Where are you from again?" he asked as they came out of the woods onto the first fields near the lake.

"I was born and raised in a town called Cawthorn, outside of Boston," she said, and that prim tone was back in her voice even as her cheeks reddened. "My parents are leading citizens. I have one sibling, an older brother. My father is the head of accounting for the largest firm. I matriculated at Boston Normal, where I obtained a teacher's certificate with a commendation for meritorious study."

Likely she thought he wouldn't understand half those fancy words. But Jesse understood.

He understood that the woman walking so stiffly beside him was far beyond his reach, socially and intellectually.

And nothing he did would ever change that.

CHAPTER THREE

OH, WHY WAS it when she was angry the number of syllables just proliferated? And truly, she had no reason to be angry with Mr. Willets. He'd protected her from a terrible storm and the dangers of the wilderness. He was protecting her even now, slowing his steps to allow her to stay at his side. He couldn't help it that he wasn't a conversationalist. Or that these shoes, which had also seemed so stylishly practical in Cawthorn, pinched harder with each step.

And he couldn't help the fact that they had been forced to spend the night together, unchaperoned.

That would have been a scandal in Cawthorn. There'd be a hurried, hushed marriage, perhaps a lengthy honeymoon to give the gossips time to turn their attentions to fresher misdeeds. But this was the frontier, and so many things were different here. Surely the citizens of Wallin Landing wouldn't be such sticklers!

"Sounds like a fine upbringing," was all he said after her tirade, for what seemed like miles. Time enough to feel the blister on her heel throbbing, her muscles aching. Time enough for the blanket to grow heavier on her shoulders. Time enough to wonder why she'd decided to run away quite this far after being left practically at the altar.

"Jesse!"

The call came from in front of them, and she managed to lift her head. More horses were cantering toward them, and she recognized Mr. Drew, his brother Simon, and Ciara's husband, Kit. The last spurred his mount to reach them first.

"Where's Ciara?" he asked, gaze darting about the road. "What happened?"

Mr. Willets held up one hand, but whether to calm the horse or the man riding it, she wasn't sure. "Ciara's fine. She stayed in Seattle. We got caught in the storm coming back."

The two Misters Wallin had reached them now as well. Especially on horseback, Mr. Drew towered over them all, even her companion. He had dark blond hair waving back from a noble brow and the deep blue eyes that seemed to mark most of his family. His brother had paler blond hair and slightly lighter eyes, and they glimmered with an intelligence that could not be denied.

"We only caught the edge of it," the elder Mr. Wallin said, voice nearly as deep as Mr. Willets'. "But, from the trees fallen along the road, you're lucky to be alive."

"It was all Mr. Willets," she felt compelled to point out as his gaze swept her way. "I could not have been in safer hands."

Mr. Willets shuffled his feet. "I took care of Lancelot and Percival."

Mr. Wallin the younger's lean face cracked in a smile. "So I see. Tie them behind Kit's horse. If you mount up behind Drew, I can take Miss Dennison." He touched the brim of his hat. "With your permission, ma'am."

Alice nodded gratefully. Because it was a shorter distance, she supposed they would not be overtaxing the horses to ride double.

Mr. Willets secured Lancelot and Percival to Kit's horse, Mr. Simon secured her chalk in his saddle bag, then Mr. Willets came to help her mount. Once more, his hands were gentle on her waist, but his gaze refused to meet hers. She was beginning to think he was shy, and that seemed rather sweet in such a large man.

They started back through the forest toward the settlement, the lake offering brief flashes through the trees on the right, the hillside rising on the left. Birds called in the woods, and she caught sight of an eagle through the gaps in the trees overhead. The air felt cool and moist against her cheeks.

"Everything all right, Miss Dennison?" Mr. Simon asked.

"I'm fine," she told his back as she clung to his waist. At least he was a married man. No one could say she was aiming to be *his* wife. "But we left the other school supplies and the wagon just outside Seattle."

"We'll send someone back for them as soon as possible," he promised.

They were all very nice, asking after her health, telling her she had been very brave. The Wallin ladies were no different when they reached the settlement a short time later. Since the day she'd first set foot in Wallin Landing, she'd admired how the community members cared for one another. Perhaps it was because so many were related by blood or marriage. Everywhere she turned, she met a Wallin. She was just glad most people seemed to have adopted her friend Katie Jo's way of discussing them, by their honorifics and first name, or it would have been easy to become confused.

Of course, the care for neighbors might have come from the small number of neighbors. Wallin Landing would have fit in one corner of Cawthorn. The mercantile was the only place to shop, and it held the post office. Houses and farms lay to the south, with a few cabins to the north. They had the Wooden Rose Inn, the school, a library, a smithy, and a dispensary. And that was about it.

But as soon as the gentlemen reined in the horses in

front of the inn, they were surrounded. Mrs. Rina, her superior, made sure Alice was tucked into her quarters at the back of the schoolhouse with a warm brick at her feet. At least the school was out for the day, so she would not have to worry her students.

Mrs. Catherine, who was a nurse, checked her temperature and pulse and proclaimed her fit. Dark-haired Nora, Simon's wife, who was a seamstress, brought her an extra quilt. Golden-haired Dottie, John's wife, brought her a book from the library to read, and blond Callie, the minister's wife, brought her a pot of beans and a pan of cornbread.

"With Ciara out, Katie Jo will likely be doing most of the cooking at the inn," she predicted.

Her friend Katie Jo McAllister was the last to stop by Alice's room that afternoon. She would have been another scandal in traditional Cawthorn, for she often dressed in flannel shirts and trousers like a man. But, Alice had learned, a kind and loyal heart beat in that generous chest.

"Sorry I didn't come sooner," Katie Jo said, perching on the edge of the bed where Alice lay, as swaddled and cosseted as if she had been back in Cawthorn. "I was helping Jesse with the cooking."

Alice leaned back into the pillow. She had somehow thought her gallant knight in shining flannel would be resting as well after their ordeal. "Mr. Willets cooks?"

Katie Jo nodded, pausing to push a lock of honey-blond hair out of her eyes. "He used to cook for the logging crew before Ciara came to take on the duties. It's pretty plain food, but it's filling."

"He seems to enjoy helping people," Alice mused.

"He does at that." Katie Jo leaned closer. "And so does Mr. Hitchcock. He's outside, fit to be tied because Mrs. Rina wouldn't let him in without your say so."

Alice dropped her gaze and picked at the covers. She

quite admired the lawyer, who had recently moved to Wallin Landing to handle the affairs of little Grace, Kit's niece, who was a considerable heiress. But every time Mr. Hitchcock spoke, so cultured, she was reminded of her traitorous fiancé, Roland.

And she didn't want to think about Roland. Ever again.

"I'm not sure I'm up to his company," she told her friend. "Would you make my excuses?"

"Sure," Katie Jo said. "I can tell him you're plumb tuckered out." She leaned closer and dropped her voice, as if she thought the dapper Mr. Hitchcock was listening at the door. "Do you want me to say the same to Mr. Bradshaw? He wanted to come riding out to find you with the others, but Mrs. Rina convinced him to stock the wood in the school instead. His boy was real worried too."

Mr. Bradshaw was the local blacksmith. He was also a fine figure of a man, and his little boy Johnny was a dear. She'd thought his interest had been confined to her as his son's teacher. If he thought to court her, she should probably nip that interest in the bud.

"If I'm too tired to see Mr. Hitchcock, I'm too tired to see Mr. Bradshaw," she told Katie Jo.

Her friend straightened. "When all the fellers suddenly started chasing me after I wore a dress to Ciara's wedding, I didn't understand their interest. But you? I know you had the gents interested in Cawthorn, and you could have even more of them here. Not every man is a low-down skunk like the one that stood you up."

The memory still rankled. "But that's the point, Katie Jo. How do you know which ones are the princes and which are the skunks?"

She shrugged. "I guess you just have to watch their actions. As far as I can tell, both Mr. Hitchcock and Mr. Bradshaw are gentlemen through and through."

Roland had seemed the same, until he'd proven himself to be someone else entirely. And she wasn't willing to risk disappointment again.

Jesse dunked a pot into the kitchen sink in time to see Logan Bradshaw and his boy leaving the school. That was one good thing about the Wooden Rose Inn. Perched as it was on the edge of a bench overlooking Lake Union, it faced the main clearing of the settlement. It was easily visible to anyone who came through, and anyone who came through was easily visible from the windows of the kitchen and big dining room.

What he couldn't understand was why he suddenly wanted to punch the blacksmith in his smiling face.

From the day he'd shot up to meet his mother's gaze, at only nine, he'd promised her and his father he'd never use his size to bully others. His strength and prowess were abilities that could bless, not hurt. Shaking his head, he started scrubbing the pot.

Kit came in from the dining room, Grace up in his arms. The little girl had hair as dark and curly as his, even though she was his orphaned niece, not his daughter. She opened her arms and reached for Jesse.

Jesse shook the water off his hands and accepted her. How many times had he held his little brothers and sisters like this? He bounced her on his hip, and Grace laughed.

"I've been thinking about what you said," his friend murmured, running a hand back through his hair. "About the smallpox and Ciara's sister. I can't leave her there, Jesse. I need to go to her."

Pain and fear reverberated in Kit's voice. Jesse shifted Grace to his other hip. "You can't. You have to think of Grace. She's already lost her ma and pa. She can't lose you and Ciara too."

He sucked in a breath. "And I can't lose Ciara."

"I know."

But he didn't, not really. Kit and Ciara loved each other deeply, and they'd only been married a month. He hadn't ever found such a love, though he'd seen it in his parents as well. Devotion, tenderness, a willingness to risk everything if it meant the other's happiness.

"She's strong," Jesse said. "She and her sister will pull through, and she'll be home before you know it."

Someone rapped at the door a moment before Mrs. Gladys Volland traipsed into the kitchen, gray curls bouncing on either side of her face. She wrinkled her long nose as if she disliked the smell of baked beans, then latched her eyes on Kit.

"Mr. Weatherly," she announced, sweeping closer, her flowered cotton skirts brushing the worn wood floor. "We are having a board meeting at the school tonight. I expect you to attend."

Kit had recently been voted on to the new schoolboard. "I don't remember a meeting scheduled for tonight," he said with a frown.

"We have urgent business to discuss," she insisted. Then she looked to Jesse. "And I need you to attend as well, Mr. Willets."

"No, no, no, no, no," Grace warbled, chanting her favorite word.

Jesse agreed completely. "But I don't have a child in the school."

She tsked. "I am aware of that, sir. You are needed for other reasons. The meeting starts at seven. Do not be late."

She swirled and stalked out.

Jesse frowned. Mrs. Volland wasn't well liked in the settlement, but her husband was attempting to bring back the old Rankin claim, and he seemed a good man. Their little girl, Mavis, who was in Alice's class, had plenty of vinegar from what he'd seen of her on the swings that hung from the trees at the edge of the schoolyard, but her mother's superior attitude likely made it hard for her to be accepted by the other parents. Against all odds, Mrs. Volland had been voted onto the new schoolboard, along with Mrs. Catherine, Mr. John, Kit, and the blacksmith.

"You know what this is about?" he asked Kit, who shook his head.

Jesse had helped build the second classroom where Alice taught, but surely they wouldn't need another room so soon. And if they did, they'd ask Drew about the cost and schedule, not him. Besides why would they hold a meeting when Alice was recuperating from the storm?

The thought of Alice set his gaze off to the school again, where a little room sat at the back. The teacher's quarters. The story went that Mrs. Rina had used the space for a time before marrying Mr. James. Since then, the room had been reserved for visitors, until Ciara had opened the Wooden Rose Inn. He could imagine Alice in a big bed now, pillows and quilts piled around her, warm and safe.

And if anyone knew he was imagining Alice in a bed of any kind, he'd be in trouble. He could feel his cheeks heating already.

But he made sure to shave, dress in his Sunday clothes, and present himself at the schoolhouse with Kit just before seven.

Mr. Bradshaw, Mrs. Catherine, and Mr. John were already there. Bradshaw was a good-sized man with dark brown hair. The scent of smoke seemed to linger around him, a hazard of his profession. And Mrs. Catherine had always made Jesse think of a queen with her pale blond hair that never seemed out of place and her piercing blue eyes that could look right through him. Sometimes he thought she knew what ailed a body simply by gazing long enough.

But Mr. John was his favorite Wallin brother after Mr. Drew. His hair was a shade of red darker than Jesse's, and he had green eyes. Supposedly, he was the only Wallin to resemble their late mother rather than their late father. He was mechanically inclined, loved to learn, and spent much of his time in the library he had founded, which reminded Jesse of his middle brother, Jacob.

For a moment, the memories of home begged to be opened. Jesse shut the door on them. He needed all his wits about him if he were to take part in this meeting.

Mrs. Catherine spotted him first, breaking off her conversation with her brother-in-law and smiling at him. "Good evening, Jesse. Did you come to see how Alice is faring?"

There was too much interest in that blue gaze. "No, ma'am."

Mrs. Catherine frowned, then her gaze went past him. With a sinking feeling, he turned to see Alice coming out of her quarters. Her eyes dipped down at the corners, but she rallied and continued forward. She'd changed into his favorite gown of hers, a blue that was nearly the color of her eyes, with fanciful white swirls along the collar, cuffs, and hem, like waves breaking on the Sound. And her hair was confined with little combs. He missed the curls.

He had no business missing the curls!

"Good evening, Mr. Willets," she said in her proper voice, lifting her chin as she passed him. "An impromptu schoolboard meeting tonight is about to commence. I'm afraid you'll have to exit the premises."

"No, he won't," Mrs. Volland announced, strutting through the schoolroom door. "I asked him to join us." She went straight to the teacher's desk at the top of the room and took the chair. Mrs. Catherine and Mr. John exchanged glances. Jesse would have thought that seat would belong to Alice, but maybe things went differently at schoolboard meetings.

"Oh?" Kit asked, squeezing his lanky frame onto the seat of one of the children's desks.

"Indeed," Mrs. Volland said, pointy nose in the air. "We are here tonight to discuss the scandalous behavior of one of our teachers."

Alice sucked in an audible breath before she lowered herself at another desk. Jesse did his best to shrink into the back of the room, but he couldn't force himself to leave.

"What exactly do you mean by that?" Mr. Bradshaw demanded, eyes narrowing. Like Jesse, he remained standing. Neither of them would fit at one of the desks.

"I have it on good authority," Mrs. Volland said as if savoring each word, "that Miss Dennison spent the night, alone, with a man!"

Alice seemed to be hunching in on herself.

"In the middle of a storm!" Mrs. Catherine protested. "With trees blocking the road. What did you expect her to do? Stumble home in the dark and rain?"

"A true lady would not have allowed herself to be out in the dark and the rain to begin with," Mrs. Volland insisted. "We cannot have a person of questionable morals teaching our children."

Alice's head came up at last. "My morals, madam, are not questionable."

"No, I suppose they aren't," Mrs. Volland sneered. "We know exactly how poor they are."

Jesse took a step forward, to do what, he wasn't sure, but Alice rose.

"If some find having the presence of mind to seek shelter in a storm offensive, I can only question their intelligence and perspicacity. I will not apologize for lacking the prescience to foresee a change in the weather. Nor will I apologize for journeying into the city to secure additional supplies for our precious students. If I am guilty of anything, it is being willing to take risks to ensure my students have the best education possible."

Kit and Mr. John nodded, Mr. Bradshaw grinned, and Mrs. Catherine applauded.

Mrs. Volland sniffed. "A fine speech, one I'm sure you have been rehearsing ever since you returned in disgrace. I have spoken with several of the other mothers, and we are all agreed that you must set an example for our children. A lady would resign, but if I must, I will insist on you being discharged."

Alice washed white.

"She shouldn't have to lose her job." Jesse was surprised to hear his own voice echoing in the quiet. "If the night she had to spend with me compromised her, we'll just get married."

CHAPTER FOUR

EVERYONE WAS ARGUING, loud and heated, but Alice heard the voices as if from a distance. Mr. Willets had just boldly announced that they would marry. Audacious! Scandalous! Unthinkable!

And yet…

If she married Jesse Willets, neither Roland nor her family could ever force her to come home. It was bad enough they kept sending telegrams. The first time Harry Yeager, one of the local loggers and her friend Katie Jo's intended, had brought one from Seattle when he'd gone to fetch the mail for the settlement, she'd told her concerned friends it was just well wishes on her new position. Kit, at least, had looked at her askance, but he hadn't questioned her. She was fairly sure she knew what he was thinking. Who sent telegrams just to say good luck? The costly things were generally reserved for jubilant news.

Or disasters.

But if she married Jesse Willets, those telegrams would likely stop. The deed would be done. No one could bully her into marrying some other man they had hand-picked for her. She would be in charge of her own destiny.

Or would she?

A husband could be a great blessing or a curse. She'd had quite enough of arranging her life to suit others. She eyed the logger across the room from her. His gaze was darting from one schoolboard member to the other, and he shifted on his feet as if he were highly tempted to bolt. He didn't look as if he had mercenary intent. If anything, he looked concerned about the uproar he'd caused.

He might be more than a foot taller than she was and likely outweighed her by close to one hundred pounds of sheer muscle, but she didn't think he'd ever bully her. From everything she'd seen, he went out of his way to be kind to everyone.

And she could probably think faster than he did if needed.

She slipped out of her seat and went to join him.

"I didn't mean to cause a fuss," he murmured, gaze still on the schoolboard, who were mostly red-faced, with arms either braced on the teacher's desk or fingers wagging. If she had been Mrs. Volland, she would likely have wilted under the fire, but the schoolboard president merely stood, just as angry and determined as the others.

"You did nothing wrong, Mr. Willets," Alice assured him. "I found your solution quite logical."

His gaze flew to hers, wide and startled. "You did?"

She nodded. "Marrying you saves both my reputation and my position. I'm grateful you were willing."

Those russet brows gathered in a frown. "And *you're* willing?"

Doubts rushed at her from every directions like gulls after a choice morsel. She raised her chin. "I am. I have found you to be an honest, hardworking, kind-hearted gentleman. A lady could do worse."

His hands rubbed at his trousers as if he needed to keep them occupied. "A lady could do a lot better. You could have your pick. Maybe we should ask around before you decide."

Was she to be put up for auction to the highest bidder? She shuddered just thinking of it. As it was, she only knew of two gentlemen who might be interested in courting her. She couldn't look across the table every evening at Mr. Hitchcock only to see someone who reminded her of everyone she'd left behind and why. And it wouldn't be right to marry Mr. Bradshaw when his son deserved a mother who loved his father.

"If you're certain, I'm certain," she told the logger. She tilted back her head to peer more closely at him. Lines crossed his forehead, and his cheeks were pale and sweaty.

"You *are* certain, aren't you, Mr. Willets?" she couldn't help asking.

Something crossed his face, a yearning she could not name. Just as quickly, it was gone, and he stood taller, as if having made a decision.

"Yes, ma'am. I'm certain. Seems you need a husband, and I'm the best man for the job."

Relief washed over her. "Then it's decided. I am honored to accept your offer." She held out her hand.

In Cawthorn, a gentleman might have brought it to his lips for a kiss in such a situation. Jesse took a hold of it, his hand dwarfing hers, and gave it a good shake, as if they'd come to a bargain.

"Alice?"

Mrs. Catherine's voice cut through the noise, and everyone else fell silent. Alice turned to find them all staring at her and Jesse. Kit and Mr. John were frowning. Mrs. Volland had her arms crossed over her chest, as if vowing not to be moved for any reason. And Mr. Bradshaw regarded Alice as if all hope had just been extinguished.

"I believe we have a solution to the problem," Alice told them all. "If that is all tonight, perhaps we could adjourn? I've had a long day, and it seems I have a wedding to plan."

She was cool as a cucumber, Jesse would give her that. Every last one of them was staring. Mrs. Volland recovered first.

"We most certainly do not have a solution," she scolded, dropping her arms. "Marriage is not an institution to be entered into lightly."

He might never have been a bully, but he recognized one when he saw one.

"No, ma'am," Jesse told her, tucking Alice's hand into his elbow. "Which is why I'll be speaking to the pastor right after services tomorrow."

Mrs. Volland's eyes narrowed. "And if he cautions you against it?"

Did she want to see Alice sent back to this Cawthorn place in disgrace? He'd offered a way to keep her at the school and in Wallin Landing, and Alice seemed to agree it was a good approach. He glanced at the other members of the board. "I don't see why he would. Do you?"

Mr. John rubbed his chin with one hand. "Levi will likely do whatever you and Alice want, Jesse."

"And you're sure this is what you want, Miss Dennison?" the blacksmith put in.

Jesse's gaze returned to his bride-to-be. Her smile was soft and almost sad. "Yes, Mr. Bradshaw. If it would satisfy the board that they have indeed hired a woman of character, I'd be happy to wed Mr. Willets."

Happy to wed him. *Him*!

"I'm sure many members of this board would consider you a woman of character regardless of whether you married Mr. Willets," Mrs. Catherine said. She gave Mrs. Volland such a look it was a wonder the other woman's hair didn't catch fire.

"Here, here," Kit said before turning his dark gaze to Jesse's. "You sure about this, Jesse?"

Kit had heard Jesse prose on about true love a time or two. Harry, the other member of their logging crew, would probably give him a good ear-jawing about stepping away from his dream. But what else could he have done? He couldn't let them discharge Alice when nothing about last night had been her fault. He was the one who hadn't driven the horses fast enough to outrun the storm. He was the one who'd refused to try to ride them in the dark with two to a horse.

Besides, he would count himself no kind of man to leave her with the blame.

"Yes," Jesse said. "I'm sure."

"Then I say this matter is settled," Mrs. Catherine declared. Once again, she looked to Mrs. Volland, as if daring her to disagree.

The two glared at each other. Mr. John took a step closer to his sister-in-law. So did Kit. Mr. Bradshaw took a step closer to Alice.

"Fine," Mrs. Volland spat, gathering up the papers she had brought with her. "The matter is settled. Next month, be prepared to discuss new history textbooks. Meeting adjourned." She stomped out of the schoolroom without another look to Alice.

Alice took a deep breath, as if the very air smelled sweeter.

Kit came over and clapped Jesse on the shoulder. "Looks like you're getting married, my friend. Congratulations."

Jesse grinned at him. "Thanks."

"And congratulations to you too, Alice," Mrs. Catherine said, coming to join them. "I know you cannot have spent much time with Jesse, but I can assure you he is an upstanding gentleman, greatly admired in the area."

Heat rushed to his face. "Thanks," he murmured, gaze falling to the black leather boots sticking out from under her skirts.

"My husband has had nothing but praise for his willingness to pitch in wherever needed," she continued, voice warm and fond. "Wallin Landing is quite fortunate to count him as a citizen."

Much more of this, and he'd be running for his family's ranch.

"Thank you, Mrs. Wallin," Alice said. "It is very good to hear that I will be marrying such a paragon."

If the floor would just crack open a little…

But he'd help put in the floor, and he knew it was sturdy. He wouldn't be able to escape the attention by melting into it. He was just glad that Mr. John moved to escort his sister-in-law home then. The blacksmith followed them out, with one last, long look at Alice. Maybe if he'd spoken his piece and married her sooner, Jesse wouldn't be standing beside her now.

Funny how he couldn't muster an ounce of regret.

Kit was putting out the lamps. "You two take your time. I'm sure you have a lot to discuss."

They did?

Panic pricked him. It must have shown on his face, for she patted his arm. "It's all right, Mr. Willets. We can discuss all the particulars after you speak to Mr. Levi in the morning. What time would you like me to be ready?"

Jesse frowned. "Ready?"

"For you to walk me to church."

Oh, right. That's what engaged couples did, walk places together. And eat together.

And talk.

Jesse swallowed. "Half past nine?"

Her smile made him warm all over. "Perfect. I'll meet you at the inn for breakfast, and we can go afterward."

She turned in a swirl of blue and white and disappeared into the teacher's quarters.

Kit handed him the last lamp. "You might need this to get back to Harry's. You sure you can make it that far?"

Jesse shook himself. "Yes. Thanks, Kit."

His friend clapped him on the shoulder again, then headed out the door. Jesse followed.

The night and forest closed in around him as he moved away from the village center. Harry's cabin was on a claim that ran along the base of the hill, which edged the main part of the settlement. It was a fine cabin, with two rooms and a stone fireplace. The plan had been for Jesse to bunk there until Harry married on Monday, at which point he'd transfer back to a small cabin on the other side of the clearing. Katie Jo and her brother Zeke were living there now.

Where was he going to bring a wife?

His shoulders sagged. He should have thought of that. His cabin was only partially finished, and he'd never get the rest done before he and Alice had to wed. Mrs. Volland likely wouldn't approve of a long engagement.

"Where have you been?" Harry greeted him as Jesse came through the door. His friend was sitting by the fire, stockinged feet out toward the warmth. "I expected you as soon as dinner was over."

"Schoolboard meeting," Jesse said, setting the lamp on the table.

Harry's brows shot up. He was a handsome feller, Harry, with hair the color of roasted chestnuts and a neat mustache and beard. He knew how to swagger too, something Jesse had never managed.

"Since when do you have to attend a schoolboard meeting?" he demanded.

"Since I agreed to marry the schoolmarm," Jesse said. "Night, Harry." He grabbed the rungs of the ladder that led up to the loft, where he'd laid out his bedding.

Harry jumped to his feet and rushed over to grab a rung too, keeping him from climbing. "Wait! You're marrying Alice Dennison?"

"Yes," Jesse said. "And I'm walking her to church in the morning."

He unpeeled Harry's fingers from the ladder and climbed to the loft.

"How did that happen?" Harry called up, but Jesse shut the trapdoor before his friend could ask him anything more. It wasn't as if he had any real answers, or at least answers he could explain even to himself.

That didn't stop his friend from peppering him with questions as they headed for the inn early the next day. Jesse finally told him the whole story, and Harry had punched his shoulder and told him he was a lucky fellow.

He didn't feel all that lucky, until he and Katie Jo had finished serving breakfast to Harry, Zeke, Kit, and Grace, and Alice appeared in the doorway of the inn. They'd put a sign in the window letting others know that the inn proper would be closed until further notice, but someone still had to feed the Wallin Landing workforce and Grace.

It was griddle cakes that morning because they were easy, and Katie Jo had only enough eggs left for them. He nearly dropped the platter on the floor when Alice smiled at him.

She was dressed in a deep blue gown embroidered all over with black thread, and the scalloped satin at the edge of the overskirt dripped beads as black and shiny as her hair. Katie Jo scooted over on the bench to make room for her at the big table, and Jesse set down the griddle cakes and promptly went to find something in the kitchen.

Something. He glanced around the space for inspiration, but all he could see was a slender figure perfectly outlined in blue.

"You bringing the preserves, Jesse?" Harry called from the main room.

Preserves. Right.

He found the black raspberry preserves Ciara had put up and carried them to the table in time to sit and respond "Amen" to the blessing Harry said over the food.

"No, no, no, no, no," Grace heralded from her tall chair near his.

"Yes, ma'am," Jesse told her with a grin before tucking in.

He managed to get three cakes down before Harry roped him into the conversation.

"So, Jesse tells me you two are getting married, Alice."

Katie Jo choked on her mouthful and had to reach for her cup of apple cider. Harry patted her back.

"It was a sensible proposal," Alice said, calmly cutting off another piece of her griddle cake.

Katie Jo managed to collect herself. "Always thought the proposal should be more than sensible," she said, looking from one to the other.

So had Jesse. He stabbed another cake and shoved it into his mouth whole before he could say anything that might get him into trouble.

Zeke helped him carry the empty plates back to the kitchen a short time later. Katie Jo might be a powerfully built female, even in the blue dress she was wearing for church today, but her brother was thin and scrawny. Jesse had heard it was because he'd ailed as a child. Mrs. Catherine was dosing him, though, and already his hollow cheeks had filled out some, and there was more color in them.

"How'd you get her to say yes?" he asked with a quick look out the door to Alice, who was talking with Katie Jo.

Because she'd been desperate, but Jesse decided not to say that aloud. "Just lucky, I guess."

Zeke shook his head in obvious admiration.

At least the sun had come out to grace the morning as Jesse escorted Alice to services. He spotted a squirrel scampering up one of the fir trees, hunting seed. The lady beside him seemed unmoved. She even walked proper, her skirts skimming the grass in graceful little eddies.

She'd put a feathered hat on her hair, and the plumes bobbed with each step.

"We should call each other by our first names," she said as they started up the hill to where the church stood on a promontory overlooking the lake. "I believe yours is Jesse."

Jesse's head bobbed like one of the feathers. "Yes, ma'am."

Her laugh was as soft as spring rain. "And you don't need to call me ma'am. I'm Alice."

"Yes, ma'am," Jesse said, and wished he could take it back.

She merely smiled at him, and the two walked into services together.

Normally, he liked worshipping in the Wallin Landing chapel. The walls and bench pews were all a nice warm wood, as was the simple cross at the altar. And Mr. Levi had a way of speaking that was easy to follow.

Today, Jesse was aware of how many gazes were aimed his way. The various Wallin ladies were smiling at him. The Wallin gentlemen were nodding. Mrs. Volland was glaring. And many of the miners, farmers, and loggers in the area were scowling.

One more eligible miss off the market. And it wasn't as if there were any others left.

Alice excused herself to go talk to two of her students after services, and he ambled up to their minister. He couldn't quite credit the stories told of Mr. Levi, the youngest Wallin brother. His curly golden hair and deep blue eyes made him look more like one of those paintings of an angel than the troublemaker his family fondly remembered. Jesse wasn't sure how to bring up the subject, but Mr. Levi wasn't about to let him off the hook.

"Mrs. Volland tells me you intend to marry," he said.

Hadn't she trusted him to keep his promise? "Yes, sir," Jesse said. "As soon as possible."

"Well, Harry's wedding is tomorrow," Mr. Levi reminded him. "And I'm sure your bride needs time to prepare. The soonest I'd advise is Thursday."

Jesse swallowed. "That sounds fine."

The minister peered closer, and Jesse did his best not to squirm. "I have to ask. Are you sure about this, Jesse? I understand you were coerced into making an offer."

He looked at Alice, who was bending to shake one of her student's hands. The little girl gazed up at her adoringly.

"Not coerced," Jesse said. "It was the right thing to do."

"You're a good man, Jesse," the minister said. "Just remember: Marriage is forever. The only way around that is having the Territorial Legislature grant you a divorce, like Doc Maynard did. I wouldn't advise it, particularly if you're trying to avoid a scandal."

"I don't aim to get divorced," Jesse promised him. "Just married."

Even if some part of him protested that he had had other plans for forever than to marry without love.

CHAPTER FIVE

NEARLY EVERYONE CONGRATULATED Alice after services, as if she were about to enter the perfect marriage. But it wouldn't be perfect. She didn't love Jesse, and he didn't love her.

Besides, perfect marriages were too highly valued. She'd thought she was destined for one, and look where that had led: disappointment, disillusionment, and derision. Her arrangement with Jesse was far more practical and manageable.

He walked her back to the school after services.

"Spoke with Mr. Levi," he said as they crossed the clearing and the sun warmed her. "He says Thursday would be a convenient day to wed."

It wouldn't be all that convenient for her. She had her teaching duties. But the school would be let off tomorrow for the wedding of Katie Jo and Harry. Perhaps Mrs. Rina would be amenable to allowing her time for her own wedding.

"I will see what I can do about arranging the afternoon off," she said. "I suppose it's too late to see about suitable attire."

His gaze dropped to the navy coat and wool trousers she had noticed he generally wore on Sundays. "This isn't suitable?"

Roland, Gerald, and her father wouldn't have worn

that suit to their own funerals, much less their weddings, but they didn't live on the frontier. It couldn't be easy for him to keep the material so clean and pressed. He didn't have a valet.

Or a wife, yet.

"Your suit should be fine," she told him. "I'll see which of my dresses is appropriate."

"Any would do." He cleared his throat as if realizing the comment sounded as if he didn't care. "That is, you look real pretty in all of them."

How nice of him to notice. Roland had always made her feel as if she must make an effort to be good enough for him. Even her mother had worried.

"You wore that dress last time you walked out with him," she'd say. "Hurry, go change into the blue before he gets here. I don't want him thinking your wardrobe is limited."

Compared to the ladies here in Wallin Landing, the small part of her wardrobe she'd brought with her was extensive, if not entirely practical, and she was beginning to realize how blessed she had been.

They had reached the schoolhouse. Jesse stopped on the stoop, gaze going everywhere but at her.

"I expect you have things you want to be doing," he said.

"I do," she told him. "Thank you for your consideration, Jesse."

"Will you sit with me for Harry's wedding tomorrow?" he asked the tree at the side of the school.

Alice smiled. "I would be delighted. But I expect I'll see you at dinner this afternoon. You will be attending the Wallin dinner, won't you?"

The Wallin family used the church hall to serve a Sunday dinner for their friends and workers. Although Alice didn't work for them per se, she had always been included. She hadn't managed to figure out how to cook over the fire in the schoolroom, except to boil water for tea and toast bread on a fork, which she did for breakfast some mornings. So she couldn't contribute to the spread of food that always filled the table along one wall. But she'd tried to help with the children or the dishes.

"Yes, ma'am." He shook his head hard and raised his chin. "Yes, Alice. I'll see you there."

He loped across the clearing so fast she might have thought a mountain lion was on his tail.

What an odd sort of fellow she was marrying. Mrs. Catherine had gone out of her way to sing his praises. He was apparently great friends with Ciara's husband and Katie Jo's intended. Perhaps she should dig a little deeper into her soon-to-be groom.

But it was difficult to get anyone at the family dinner to talk of anything except tomorrow's wedding.

"James went into Seattle to see if he could safely extradite Ciara," Mrs. Rina confided as the Wallin ladies took a moment at the long center table. The fathers were playing games with the children, and the bachelors, Jesse and Harry, were helping Katie Jo with the dishes. "I'm hoping they'll return by this evening."

Ciara would likely be shocked to find Alice and Jesse engaged, with another wedding planned later in the week. And Alice should write to her family and let them know.

After she was safely wed and they could do nothing about it.

"That's excellent news," Mrs. Catherine said with a nod. "Katie Jo will have her bridesmaid in place. What of the other arrangements?"

"Frisco and Sutter rounded up some flowers from the lakeshore for the church," Mrs. Callie put in. "And Katie Jo and I settled on music for the service."

"Simon will play for the reception," Mrs. Nora added. "And I finished Katie Jo's dress last night."

The other ladies thanked the seamstress for her hard work.

Mrs. Catherine reached out and patted Alice's hand. "And as soon as the ceremony is done, we can start planning your wedding."

"Thursday, I heard," Mrs. Callie put in. As the minister's wife, she would know such things.

"Yes," Alice said as the rest of them stared at her. "I was hoping I might have the afternoon off, Mrs. Rina."

"Take the entire day off," she said. "I'll close the school at noon. Your students will want to see you happy."

She wasn't sure she would be happy, but she had every confidence she could find contentment. No more Roland. The freedom to take charge of her life.

Jesse walked her back to the schoolhouse again as daylight faded. Other families were moving toward the various cabins sprinkled around the settlement. Mrs. Catherine and Mr. Drew passed them, hand in hand, and she spotted Mr. James taking a moment to press a kiss to Mrs. Rina's cheek. Something tugged at her, a longing she'd thought she'd left behind with the rest of her dresses.

"I hope we can grow more comfortable with each other," she murmured to her silent escort as she stopped at the door. "I would like to think we can become friends, at least."

"Friends." He latched onto the word as if it were a lifeline. "I'd like to be your friend, Alice."

"Good." She should say more, but now she was the awkward one. Surely this close to the wedding, he might expect to peck her on the cheek too. She didn't know him well enough to allow that sort of intimacy.

Well, Alice, if you don't know him well enough for that, why are you marrying him!

He must have seen the shudder that went through her, because he stepped back.

Roland had always told her what to do, how to behave, and her family had encouraged her to go along with him. The honor of having their daughter be courted by the scion of the most powerful family in the area was simply too good to forego.

This time, she was the one in control. She decided what happened and when. Anything else just led to heartache.

"And, as friends," she made herself say, "I just want to be certain you understand this is a marriage of convenience."

He frowned. Perhaps he didn't know the word.

"Platonic," she tried.

His frown grew.

"We will have separate rooms and separate beds." Her cheeks felt as if she'd stood too close to the fire.

"Always?"

She swallowed. "For as long as need be. I do hope that doesn't change your mind about our agreement."

He regarded her a moment, and she caught herself holding her breath. Finally his brow cleared. "No, ma— Alice. I said I'd be your husband. I stand by my word. Night." Once more he turned on his heel and left her, but this time, his steps seemed slower, as if she'd stolen his joy.

So, theirs wasn't to be a real marriage. He had known their arrangement was odd, but he hadn't expected it would be that odd. Couldn't very well sire a passel of children in a marriage of convenience. It would be no different than bunking with Harry and Kit.

Except neither Harry nor Kit made him think of soft smiles and tender looks.

He squared his shoulders as he entered the inn. He'd lived with four sisters growing up. He knew what it meant to have hair ribbons and embroidery hoops lying about. He even knew how to lace a corset. Maybe it wouldn't be so bad.

His conversation with Ciara put a lie to that thought.

She and James returned that evening as Jesse was putting away the last of the dishes the Wallins had borrowed from the inn for Sunday dinner. She went straight to the cabin Kit and the Wallins had built her to the north of the inn, but Jesse was surprised when she bustled into her establishment a short time later.

"Evening, Jesse," she said as if she hadn't been away on a potentially dangerous mission. "I just want to set up for breakfast."

"No smallpox?" Jesse asked, putting the last dish in place on the sideboard by the sink and pump.

"No, praise the Lord!" Ciara tied her apron about her middle as if girding herself for battle. "That dread disease is still confined to the south, we hope. Maddie had a rash that cleared up, and her other symptoms are easily explained." She winked at him. "She and Michael are expecting!"

He felt as if she'd landed a punch to his gut. "Well, that's good news."

"It is indeed. They've wanted a child for so long."

And Alice didn't want any.

Jesse leaned against the sideboard as Ciara bustled about checking her bread starter and the flour in the sack.

"Did Mr. James tell you about me and Alice?" he asked.

In the act of studying the loaf of sugar, she turned his way, face sad. "Yes. I need to speak with her about all that. How are you holding up, Jesse?"

Jesse shrugged. "I'm fine."

"Are you?" Ciara straightened and peered closer. "I was under the impression Alice scared you a little."

Terrified him, more like. All that culture and education. All those fancy clothes. He and Alice had nothing in common. Well, maybe just a desire to help others.

"She says we can be friends," he allowed.

Ciara nodded. "Well, that's a start."

It felt more like an end to Jesse.

But he rallied the next day. It was impossible not to feel happy when Harry and Katie Jo looked so full of joy as they stood at the front of the church and said their vows before family and friends. Harry looked fit to pop the buttons right off his new coat as he walked Katie Jo back down the aisle in her rose-colored skirts.

Next to Jesse, Alice was watching the couple too, face soft and wistful, like she hoped for such a love. She'd worn her dress with the puffy sleeves today, the lustrous material a little more purple than her eyes. It struck him that she ought to have a man beside her she could admire, who made her smile like Katie Jo was smiling. Who would protect her and honor her all the days of his life.

And he'd said he'd be that man. He'd never gone back on his word in his life. He wasn't going to start now. Was there a way he could get his bride to fall in love with him?

The thought seemed taller than Mount Rainier and wider than the ocean that lay beyond the Straits of Juan de Fuca.

As the other guests filed out of the church after the happy couple, heading for the hall next door, he held out his arm and felt Alice put her dainty little hand on it. "Would you dance with me at the reception?"

Her dark lashes fluttered. "I'd be delighted."

He liked dancing. He could stomp his feet and clap his hands with the best of them, and every lady who had partnered him had always thanked him with a glowing smile, as if they were pleased as well. Waltzes, reels, line dances, he knew them all. Ma had seen to it.

"And how will your sisters learn if you don't help?" she'd say to him and his brothers. His closest brother, Jack, had always thought himself above such things. "Besides, you'll want to dance at your wedding someday."

And now his wedding was a few days away. No time for Ma and Pa to get here to see it. They'd be so disappointed. He could only hope they'd understand the necessity of it and still be proud of him.

He wouldn't have minded partnering Alice on all the dances, but he knew it wasn't fair to keep her to himself, even with them being officially engaged. Gals were few enough that they were generally kind about switching partners. He wasn't sure how he was going to feel watching other men dance with his Alice, though.

He took the first dance, a reel that had him swinging her around the hall. She must have been having a good time, for the sweetest dimple appeared on either side of her petal pink lips. Made a fellow forget anything else but her smile existed.

Still, he managed to surrender her to Kit for the second dance. When Mr. Drew took the third, Jesse thought he might make it through the afternoon after all.

But Dixon Hitchcock approached Alice about the fourth dance, head bowed as if he were petitioning a magistrate. Jesse stiffened. The lawyer looked real nice, with his light brown hair all shiny and his trousers and coat of fine wool. He was smart and polished too, like Alice. Jesse had heard Ciara say Alice actually enjoyed his company. They'd walked out a time or two on a Sunday. Was he about to poach Jesse's gal?

"I won't have time to make you a suit before Thursday, Jesse," Mrs. Nora said, sidling up to him before he could step forward and offer himself for the dance instead. "But if you need anything mended, I'd be happy to help."

Jesse tore his gaze away from where the lawyer was leading Alice onto the floor to focus on the woman beside him. She was one of the shortest of the Wallin ladies, with gray threading through dark hair that tended to go every which way. "Very kind of you, ma'am, but I generally keep my clothes mended."

She smiled at him. "You're very self-sufficient. I'm sure Alice will come to appreciate that."

It would be nice if she appreciated something about him.

He grimaced as Mr. Simon's wife moved on. Alice had always thanked him for the times he'd helped her. She had obviously appreciated his efforts that night in the storm and his offer to marry her now. He needed to shake himself out of this dark mood. This was a wedding reception, not a wake!

"Has Alice mentioned flowers?" Now it was Mrs. Dottie at his side. She had to be one of the prettiest of the Wallin wives with her golden curls. "I'm not sure what we can find. Frisco and Sutter picked the last of the pearly everlasting for the wedding today."

"There's some holly with berries at the edge of Harry's claim," Jesse offered. "Might be some color, if that's the sort of thing you want."

She beamed. "That could be perfect! I'll check with Alice when I can catch her between dances." She went on her way, and Mrs. Callie stepped into her place. Though she wasn't much bigger than Mrs. Nora and more slenderly built, she reminded him of his sisters, forthright, sure of herself.

"What are you thinking for music for the service?" she asked. "I know two songs folks seem to like for weddings. Catherine told me they're called the Wedding March and the Bridal Chorus. They were played for a princess in England, and everyone's been playing them since. Do you think Alice would like either of them?"

"You'd have to ask her," Jesse said. Now Dixon Hitchcock was twirling Alice, her skirts a purple blur. Her laughter floated on the strains of Mr. Simon's violin, and his fists clenched.

"She said yes to you," Mrs. Callie reminded him as if she'd seen his reaction. "She could have had her pick."

"She still can," Jesse said before he thought better of it.

Mrs. Callie frowned at him. "You want to marry her or not?"

Until that moment, he hadn't actually thought about whether he *wanted* to marry Alice. She was pretty as a picture; she was sweeter than honey. Her students adored her. Every bachelor in the area admired her. But he hadn't pursued her because it had seemed plain to him that they would not suit, and getting to know her better had just proven that point. Only the storm and the accusations against her had made him offer his help.

Did he want to marry Alice? Even if he never won her love? Even if all she offered was a friendship?

The answer inside him was swift and hard.

"Yes, ma'am," he told Callie. "Best I go collect my gal."

CHAPTER SIX

ALICE HAD ATTENDED a number of society weddings over the years, but she couldn't recall anyone looking as happy as Katie Jo had looked as she had walked down the aisle on Harry's arm. Her friend positively glowed, and she'd danced with the same joy.

Alice hadn't sat out a single dance at the reception either, and everyone had been so kind. She'd feared Jesse might want to monopolize her given their engagement, but he'd been just attentive enough. He didn't puff up as Roland used to do when she danced with someone else, he brought her cider between dances, he sat with her while Katie Jo and Harry's other friends offered toasts and well wishes, and he had danced with her no more than twice.

She was a little surprised that they had been her favorite dances of the day.

The first had been a reel that was far more energetic than the ones she'd danced back home. In fact, she couldn't imagine her brother or Roland making it through the song without begging fatigue afterward. Mr. Simon's bow had been fraying as he played the last note, and several of the men had fanned themselves with one hand.

Jesse had just grinned at her. "Mighty fine dancing, Miss Dennison, that is, Alice."

"Mighty fine indeed," Alice had told him with a smile.

The second had been a waltz, which was often reserved for engaged or married couples. Alice had danced it in Cawthorn during her lengthy engagement with Roland, but she was a little surprised Jesse knew the steps. Roland had always waltzed far apart for propriety's sake, his gaze going more to those who were watching than her. Jesse guided her in graceful circles, holding her almost reverently, as if she were impossibly precious and dear.

"That was wonderful," she told him when the last strains faded. "Wherever did you learn to dance like that?"

He seemed to have forgotten he was still holding her, for he made no move to release her. "Ma taught all of us boys to dance. She said that way our sisters would always have partners and so would our brides." His cheeks were pinking again.

"What a very sensible mother," she said. "I hope I have an opportunity to meet her soon."

All color fled. "They can't be here in time for the wedding. I have to write." He dropped his arms and stepped back as if intending to rush off and do it that very moment.

Alice lay a hand on his arm. "I'd be happy to help, if you'd like."

A smile hinted. "Yes, ma'am."

The reception ended just before dark. Alice offered to stay and help clean up, but Ciara waved her away.

"You have enough to think about," she said, giving her hand a squeeze. "But we need to catch up soon."

"Agreed," Alice said. "And thank you."

Jesse walked her back to the schoolhouse as the evening crept in. That's what gentlemen did, after all, walk their sweethearts places like church and weddings. She nearly grimaced at the thought of sweethearts. If she couldn't manage that, how could she manage thinking of herself as a wife?

She had to try.

"I suppose in a few days we'll be walking home to your cabin," she ventured.

He jerked to a stop on the grass of the clearing and stared at her. "I don't have a cabin."

"I'm sure I heard when I first arrived that you were almost finished building one," Alice told him, confused. "That was nearly a month ago."

"I was building one," he said. He raised his head. "I *am* building one. I just haven't finished it yet."

"Oh." That was a problem, but a solution immediately presented itself. "Well, I suppose we'll have to live in the inn until you're done, then."

He shook his head, dashing her hopes. "Can't. As soon as Ciara returned, she opened it to paying customers, and Kit says they'll be full by tomorrow night."

"Where are you staying now?" she asked, frowning. "Perhaps we could stay there."

"I moved into the old Wallin cabin to the north with Zeke McAllister. I don't think he'd cotton to having a married couple bunking with him, and there's only one bed as it is."

Panic nibbled at her. "Well, we can hardly both live in my quarters! It only has one bed too."

"I'll see what can be done," he promised.

Roland had made promises too—to marry her, to love and honor her, to raise a family, to elevate her family in local society. He hadn't kept a single one.

Yet if she was to marry Jesse, she had to find a way to trust him, at least in the small things.

This didn't seem so small.

She drew in a breath. "Very well. Good night, Jesse."

"Night, Alice." He turned and ambled across the clearing to disappear into the woods at the northern edge.

She tossed and turned that night, and the fire was

unobliging the next morning, to the point that she had to poke her head into the other room and request a moment of Frisco's and Sutter's time.

"Happy to help, ma'am," Frisco said while his twin brother began rearranging the pitiable pile of wood she'd placed in the hearth.

"And we understand why you couldn't bring back sweets from your trip to Seattle like you promised," Sutter put in.

She'd wondered whether Jesse could keep a promise, and here she was guilty of breaking one! Between the storm and her upcoming marriage, she'd completely forgotten.

"I apologize, gentlemen," she told them both. "Mrs. Haggerty's bakery was closed. I'll speak to Ciara and see if we can find a suitable substitute."

The two grinned at each other.

She managed to make it through the school day and stood at the door, watching her class skip off across the clearing for their homes. A few of the mothers who came to collect their children gave her a look, as if still wondering about her, but she kept her head high and her smile pleasant.

Then Mr. Bradshaw approached. He wore the smock from his work, coated with smoke and smudges, but his dark brown hair looked freshly combed.

"Give that swing a try," he told his son, and the boy scampered off to the big cedar at the side of the school, where Kit had erected swings.

"Have you a concern, Mr. Bradshaw?" Alice asked. "I can assure you that John is a model student."

He spared his son a smile of pride. "I'm not surprised. He's a model son as well." He looked back at Alice, and his smile faded. "I wanted to say that I didn't agree with the decision at the schoolboard meeting last week. You did nothing wrong. You shouldn't be forced to marry."

"Thank you," she said, touched. "But I fear Mrs. Volland and others like her would continue to tarnish my reputation if I did otherwise. I would not want to jeopardize the children's faith in me. I'm simply grateful Mr. Willets was understanding."

His gaze brushed hers. "I could give you an alternative."

He was going to ask her to marry him. Gratitude warred with aversion. He was nearly as strong as Jesse and very likely smarter. She adored his son. If he could raise such a sweet, well-mannered boy, he likely was a good father and would make a good husband again.

But Jesse's face came to mind. Grinning after that reel, tender during that waltz. And forgetful and shy and hesitant. She might need a husband, but she was beginning to believe that he needed someone to look out for him. It was a fair trade.

"Thank you," she said. "You will never know how much you honor me. But I agreed to Mr. Willets' proposal. I will abide by that agreement."

He nodded before going to fetch his son.

"I seem to have a knack for disappointing people," Alice told Ciara that evening when they finally had a chance to talk after the dinner service. Her friend had dived back into her duties at the inn, which included cooking breakfast and dinner, keeping the place clean for guests and customers, and caring for Grace, who was just starting to toddle around the room. Kit had her on the floor now, building fortresses with blocks that Grace delighted in knocking onto the colorful rag rug created by the first Mrs. Wallin.

"You haven't disappointed anyone that I know," Ciara protested, pouring her another cup of hot cider.

Alice blew the fragrant steam away. "Frisco and Sutter, for starters," she said after taking a sip. "I promised them sweets from Seattle. I don't suppose you could help?"

"I'm making cinnamon rolls for breakfast tomorrow," she said. "I'll save two for them."

Alice sighed, feeling as if a weight had slid off her shoulders. "Thank you." Then she lowered her voice. "But they aren't the only ones I've disappointed. I can't help thinking about my parents and brother, my friends. Pretty much everyone in Cawthorn let me know it was my fault that Roland decided to wed another."

"I never met your Roland," Ciara said, pouring her own cup. "But I can't like him. He sounds like a bully and a lout and entirely obsessed with what others think of him. No offense."

Alice shrugged. "None taken. At the time, I was just so stunned that he'd even look at me. He and Gerald, my brother, had been friends since their days at a private school together, but I was just the little sister, thinking myself destined to be a teacher. And my family didn't move in nearly as high a circle as his."

"He knew a diamond when he saw one," Ciara said, cradling her cup. "He just didn't value it enough. You'll be far better off with Jesse."

Jesse had eaten and taken off for the cabin with Zeke McAllister, so she had no fear he might overhear. "Will I? Everyone keeps saying he's such a paragon. He seems a decent sort, but he hardly speaks!"

"You just need to draw him out," Ciara said, settling back in the chair.

"I'm not sure there's much to draw," Alice confessed.

Ciara smiled. "You might be surprised. It seems to me that Jesse has hidden depths."

And wouldn't that be nice if he did?

The door opened just then, and the Wallin ladies marched into the inn.

"We have two days to finish planning your wedding," Mrs. Catherine announced as they all spread their calico and wool skirts to join Ciara and Alice around the biggest table in front of the window. "So we decided to meet."

Ciara cast Alice a look and promptly went for the kitchen, likely for more cups and cider. Kit and Grace made themselves scarce. Alice almost wished she could do the same, but she could only be thankful these ladies were willing to help her.

"Thank you all so much," she said, meeting each gaze in turn, from Mrs. Callie, who was near her own age, to Mrs. Rina, her superior.

"I'm afraid we can only do so much this quickly," Catherine confessed from where she'd sat at the head of the table. Alice had noticed Mrs. Catherine generally had the run of any committee she was on, very likely because she was level-headed, kind-hearted, and organized. Mrs. Volland had only taken precedence on the schoolboard.

"Drew has a simple chest he hadn't carved yet," she continued. "I propose we fill it with things Alice and Jesse will need to start their lives together."

The other women all nodded as Ciara returned with a tray of cups.

Alice raised her hand, and Mrs. Catherine smiled at her. "You don't have to ask permission to speak, dear. This is your wedding."

She could feel her cheeks heating. "I truly appreciate the offer, but I'm not sure where we'd put the chest, much less use what's in it. Jesse tells me he doesn't have a cabin."

They all looked to Ciara.

"He has a cabin," she clarified, setting down the tray. "From what Kit tells me, it has a roof and four walls, but not much else."

Mrs. Catherine clucked her tongue and wrote something on the paper in front of her. "We'll see about that. Let's focus on the ceremony and reception for now. Nora, what do you think can be done?"

Mrs. Nora gave Alice a commiserating smile. "No time to sew a new dress, alas. But I have some lovely lace left over from Katie Jo's veil. I can make one for you."

"I have some silk flowers," Mrs. Dottie put in. "White rose buds. We can use them as a band for your hair."

Alice smiled at them both. "That sounds lovely. Thank you."

"And of course Simon would be happy to play at the reception," Mrs. Nora said to the group.

"Alice and I have already talked about what she wants for music in the service," Mrs. Callie put in.

Mrs. Catherine noted all that on her paper. "Excellent. What about decorations for the hall?"

"That matter is resolved," Mrs. Rina said with a nod to Mrs. Dottie. "We have some lovely holly we can sprinkle around. It will be very festive."

"Jesse thought of it," Mrs. Dottie confided.

He had? She wasn't sure why she was surprised. He must know the forest far better than she did. In November, it wasn't likely they'd find flowers. This was a good alternative.

"And Katie Jo and I will cook for the reception," Ciara put in, bringing back the cider.

Alice glanced around. All the women were smiling fondly at her, obviously so pleased to be of service in making the day special. "This is so sweet of you. I don't know what to say."

"Just say what you like and don't like," Mrs. Rina told her. "Otherwise, I fear we are all too good about simply doing what we think is best."

They clarified a few things with her, including songs and food for the reception, then Mrs. Rina walked her back to her quarters.

"You'll make a lovely bride," she promised with a kind smile. "And I'll be praying for a happy marriage."

Alice nodded before shutting the door and setting the bar into place.

She wandered into her room, memories tugging. Everything about this marriage with Jesse was different from the one she'd originally planned.

"Oysters," her mother had said. "We must have some for your reception. And those cunning little petit fours."

"Roland is very fond of crab," Gerald had put in. "We should probably have some crabcakes as well."

No one had asked her preferences. Her mother had chosen her dress. Her father had chosen the music to be played at the reception. She had merely been expected to smile and look pleasant. Sometimes she thought that was all Roland had expected of her too, until the end.

"But why?" she'd begged him when he'd come to tell her he was going to marry someone else after all. "We courted for two years, and we've been engaged for one. What have I done to give you a disgust of me?"

"You are entirely too pliable, Alice," he'd said. "There's no spark, no fire. I need more from a wife."

She had stood there on the porch, stunned, as he'd turned and walked away. And her mother and father had insisted it was all her fault for allowing the wealthiest bachelor in town to slip through her fingers.

Well, the choices were all hers now. She'd chosen to answer an advertisement for a schoolteacher in the settlement of Wallin Landing north of Seattle in Washington Territory. She'd chosen to cross the country with no more than a trunk and a valise. She'd chosen to marry a man she hardly knew.

The consequences, of course, were all hers too.

Jesse sat at the table in the cabin he was sharing with Zeke, lamplight glowing on the piece of paper and pencil in front of him. How could he explain his marriage to his parents?

"Love, Jesse," his mother would say to him. "That's the only good reason to get married. Don't you listen to what others say." Her gaze would go to his father, tenderness and still a little awe written in every line of her face.

"I understand you want to walk your own path," his father had said when Jesse had decided to move north as a logger. "Just remember it's better to walk it with someone you love. You find a gal you admire who admires you right back. That's the only way to be happy."

Alice didn't love him, and, at times, he wasn't sure she admired much about him. He had hoped love would grow between them, but he didn't put any faith in it if she was determined to remain friends only.

Still, he had to tell his family. They'd be hurt enough as it was to miss the wedding. Unfortunately, a letter would never reach the ranch with enough time for them to travel to Seattle by Thursday. With a sigh, he took up his pencil and began writing.

"Whatcha doing?" Zeke asked, slinging a leg over the bench beside the table that stood in the middle of the bottom floor of the cabin. He'd offered to sleep on a pallet along one wall, but Jesse had insisted that he take the bed in the loft. The kid was sickly, after all. Jesse didn't mind bunking on the floor. Most beds weren't built for his frame anyway. At least he could stretch out.

"Writing a letter to my family," he explained. "About the wedding."

"Katie Jo's sure was nice," Zeke said, leaning his chin on his hands. "I want a bigger one for my wedding. Everyone in the settlement can come."

Jesse smiled at him. "You fixing to marry soon?"

"Nah." He was off the bench and moving toward the hearth. "Who'd marry me? I gotta get healthy first." He shot Jesse a grin over his shoulder. "Then watch out, ladies of Wallin Landing!"

If only Jesse had that confidence. He bent to his work. When he finished, he studied the words again. Something was off, but he couldn't put his finger on it.

Then again, he knew someone who was real good with words.

CHAPTER SEVEN

WEDNESDAY MORNING, ALICE shook off her lingering memories and focused on her students. She had five boys and three girls, and she'd noticed the two oldest girls, Mavis Volland and Mary Wallin, Catherine and Drew's daughter, had begun to treat Anna Kincaid, the youngest, as if she were a baby doll placed in the school for their amusement. They tended to tell her where to stand and what to do, as if she was allowed no ideas of her own. It was a bit too much like Alice's upbringing.

"We are going to change seating," she announced that day, and the two older girls as well as some of the boys exchanged glances.

Davy Wallin, the other child of Catherine and Drew in her class, raised his hand. "May I sit with Johnny?"

John Bradshaw's eyes brightened.

"Yes," Alice agreed.

Before she could explain that she intended to group the children by age, two more hands shot up.

"I want to sit next to Mary," Mavis announced before Alice had even acknowledged her. "And Anna."

Anna's lower lip began to tremble.

"And I want to sit by Anna too," Mary said. "And Mavis."

Anna's little shoulders slumped.

"Gather your things and stand up," Alice said. "Mary and Mavis, you may take the seats in front of the chalkboard."

Mavis raised her chin and marched to her spot. Mary slid in beside her with a giggle.

"David and John, you will be right behind them."

The boys grinned at each other before jockeying for a spot.

"Peter and Jacob, across from them if you please."

The seven and six year olds didn't argue as they took their seats.

Anna was watching her. Alice went to stand next to Lars Wallin, the youngest boy in her class. He was the son of Simon and Nora, and she had noticed he seemed to have inherited his mother's kind heart.

"Lars," she said. "I have a very important assignment for you."

His blue eyes widened.

"I am going to place you next to Anna. As a gentleman, I know you will help her."

"Yes, Miss Dennison," he said, dropping his gaze.

Already she heard whispering. Alice speared the two oldest boys with a look. "And I expect the rest of the class to help Lars with his assignment. We are here to learn, not to gossip."

Immediately the whispers dissipated, like smoke in the wind.

"Anna and Lars, you may take your places at the desk in front of mine."

Eyes shining, Anna marched to the front of the class and slid in next to Lars, who gave her an encouraging smile.

She'd thought that might be the most challenging part of her day, but she found Mrs. Volland waiting outside the school when Alice released her students.

"There you are," she declared as if she'd expected Alice

to be elsewhere on a school day. "We must talk." She pushed past her into the school.

Given that she had only this afternoon to prepare for her wedding, Alice might have attempted to suggest another time to a parent, but she could hardly refuse the schoolboard president. She followed the lady inside and took up a rag to start erasing the day's work from the chalkboard. "How may I be of assistance, Mrs. Volland?"

"I believe you have made a grave error," the lady said, taking a seat at Alice's desk.

Alice tried not to bristle. She studied the remaining numbers on the board. "Oh? I was under the impression that multiplication tables marched along rather predictably."

Mrs. Volland peered at the board a minute as if trying to multiply in her head, then gave it up and waved an airy hand. "Very likely they do. No, I speak of this decision to marry Mr. Willets."

Alice's hand froze on the rag. "Is there something about Mr. Willets I don't know?"

"Very likely a great deal," Mrs. Volland told her. "He's a rather secretive fellow, isn't he? He doesn't say much. Keeps to himself."

She knew him even less well than Alice! "A man who values his own **counsel** is often wise," she said, rubbing out another set of numbers. A shame she couldn't wipe away her problems so easily.

"And just as often a fool," Mrs. Volland countered. "I would hate to have you marry so far beneath yourself."

Alice stiffened. She set down the rag carefully, counting to five. But the words came out nonetheless. "Jesse Willets is an upstanding member of this community, admired by any with the sagacity and perspicuity to recognize his many sterling qualities. As his affianced bride, I cannot stand by and allow you to slander his impeccable reputation."

Mrs. Volland blinked. "Are you saying you actually like the fellow?"

Alice met her gaze straight on. "I like him very much indeed."

"Well." Mrs. Volland rose in a crackle of cotton. "I simply wanted you to know that you don't have to marry him if you don't want to. You could always quit."

She waited expectantly.

Alice made herself smile. "Thank you so much for dropping by. I shan't keep you."

With a huff, Mrs. Volland stalked out.

Alice stared after her, frowning. She'd been raised in a town puffed up with pride. She'd thought she understood the schoolboard president's indignation that their new teacher had compromised herself.

But something more seemed to be at work. Why was Gladys Volland so determined to see the last of her?

Jesse finished his work early on Wednesday and ventured in to the settlement for the schoolhouse. Alice was seeing her students off. She stood on the stoop, smiling with such tenderness his heart caught. She knew something about love. Why withhold it where it would matter most, in her marriage?

Then he spotted Mrs. Volland, waiting like a cougar before a pack of deer. He slowed his steps as the woman pushed past Alice into the school.

He was a little too large for eavesdropping, but he had to own he was curious.

Lars Wallin, Mr. Simon's boy, was on the swing, kicking at the ground and not making much progress. Jesse ambled closer.

"You need a hand?"

Lars shook his head. Like his father, he had pale blond hair and light blue eyes. "Just thinking."

Jesse nodded. "Me too."

He frowned. "What about?"

"Getting married tomorrow," Jesse said. "Makes a man take stock."

Lars nodded. "Women," he said with a sigh.

Jesse tried to hide his surprise. "You got girl problems?"

Lars looked up into the tree branches. "I have to sit with Anna."

"She trouble?"

Lars wrinkled his nose as he lowered his head. "No. She's real nice. She's just little and needs help."

"Then I reckon Miss Alice chose the right man for the job."

"She said I was a gentleman," he allowed, as if he wasn't sure that was a compliment.

"You sure are," Jesse told him. "Just like your father and your uncles."

He brightened. "That's right." He hopped off the swing. "Thanks, Mr. Jesse." With a wave, he headed for the path up the hill to where his family farm lay.

Mrs. Volland stalked out of the school just then, all but slamming the door behind her. "Stubborn, ungrateful…" She stopped when she must have spotted Jesse and put on a smile that sent a chill through him.

"Mr. Willets! I'm certain *you'll* be able to help."

For one of the few times in his life, he wished his parents hadn't encouraged that trait in him. "What can I do for you, ma'am?"

"I have been thinking about that schoolboard meeting," she said, drawing closer, head cocked like a hen that spots the corn coming. "You were very gallant to step in and offer to marry Miss Dennison, but you don't have to."

Disappointment vied with relief. "You change your mind about what happened in that storm?"

She tsked. "No, certainly not. Miss Dennison's reputation

was irreparably damaged. I simply meant you shouldn't feel the need to sacrifice yourself on her behalf."

"I was alone with her in the storm," Jesse said with a shrug. "Seems as if my reputation would be damaged too."

She rolled her eyes. "Men are not held to the same standards, sir."

"They ought to be."

He didn't realize he'd said those words aloud until her chin came up.

"You needn't be argumentative," she complained. "Simply tell Miss Dennison you've changed your mind, and you can go about your life. And I will make sure that she ends her employment in Wallin Landing."

Something was wrong. She was so determined, gazing up at him as if he were her last hope.

"I don't see how Alice could have offended you," he said. "She's nice to everyone. Why are you so ready to discharge her?"

She flamed. "I'm sure I have no idea what you're talking about." She dusted her hands together. "I have done my Christian duty and given you the ability to distance yourself from all this. Don't blame me when it comes off badly." She swept off.

Bemused, Jesse went to knock at the schoolhouse door.

Alice whipped it open. "I refuse!"

Jesse reared back so far he nearly toppled off the stoop. "You decided not to marry me?"

"Oh, Jesse, no!" she said, seizing his arm. "I'm looking forward to our wedding."

She was? He felt as if the world had somehow tipped to one side while he was working, and no one had thought to tell him. The schoolboard president trying to discharge the schoolteacher? Alice actually wanting to marry him?

She drew him into the school and shut the door soundly behind him. "Forgive me for raising my voice. I thought you were Mrs. Volland." She made a face. "And I certainly shouldn't be raising my voice to her either."

"She brings it on herself," Jesse acknowledged, moseying up to the desk. "Did she talk to you too?"

"Yes," she said, sweeping up to the chalkboard and commencing to give it a good wipe, as if she'd like to do away with the schoolboard president as nicely. Then she paused and looked at him, frown gathering. "You said *too*. Did she talk to you?"

He nodded. "Wanted me to call off the wedding."

She rocked back on her heels. "Well. She said the same to me. And did she tell you that she'd discharge me if we did?"

"Yes."

She shook her head. "She truly must despise me."

Jesse snorted. "No one could despise you, Alice."

Pink popped into her cheeks before she turned her back on him and finished with the board. "You might be surprised. Now, what brought you this way, if not Mrs. Volland's interference?"

He pulled the letter from his pocket. "You offered to help me write to my parents."

She turned to face him again, smile once more sunny and bright. "Why, I'd be delighted. Come sit with me."

He started forward, but the schoolroom door opened with a bang, and he whirled, keeping himself in front of Alice for protection. Sutter Murphy waved a half-eaten cinnamon roll at him.

"Thank you, Miss Dennison!" he caroled.

"Me too!" Frisco's voice echoed from the yard.

"Someone got a reward," Jesse mused.

"One friend thanking another," Sutter informed him, face turning solemn.

"You and your brother are very welcome," Alice assured him, stepping up beside Jesse. "Run along now, if you please. Mr. Willets and I have work to do."

He grinned. "I know the kind of work courting folks do. Kissing!"

Alice flamed, but he darted out the door before she could respond.

"He means no harm," Jesse said.

"Very likely." She went to sit at her desk and beckoned him to pull up a stool that stood nearby. At least it was large enough to hold him.

Alice spread his letter out on her desk and gazed down at it. "Now, what have we here? *Dear Ma and Pa.*" She glanced up, brow puckering. "A very good salutation, but do you not call them Mother and Father?"

"No."

"Well, then, we'll leave that." Her gaze returned to the paper. "*I'm getting married on Thursday.* Perhaps a bit blunt. What about 'I would like to inform you that I will be getting married this Thursday'?"

It sounded a little formal to him, but he nodded. "That would be fine."

She noted something on the paper. "What's next? *Sorry you won't be able to come. We had to marry in a hurry because Alice was in trouble.*" She stopped, chest starting to heave. "*Alice was in trouble!* You make me sound like a fallen woman!"

Jesse held up his hands. "I meant no disrespect."

She bent her head and slashed her pencil across his words, saying them aloud as she went. "'I apologize that I was unable to send you word in time to attend. The young lady I am marrying must work as a schoolteacher and cannot take off any day she chooses. I hope to introduce you to her as soon as possible. I pray that all is well with you there. Your devoted son, Jesse.' There!" She shoved the paper at him.

They would never believe he'd written that. In fact, they might think she'd taken him hostage.

Which she rather had.

He carefully refolded the hatched paper. "I'll rewrite it in my own hand. Thank you, Alice, for your help."

Her face softened as her breathing returned to normal. "You're very welcome. I hope we can rely on each other, Jesse."

"Me too. See you at dinner." He rose and left before he could say something else she might find objectionable.

He recopied the letter and took it to the mercantile for posting. Mr. James accepted it with a wry grin. "Bit late to send an invitation, my lad. You're marrying tomorrow, or had you forgotten?"

Mr. James was the tease in the family, just like Jesse's brother Jeremy was the tease in the Willets' family. Jesse appreciated anyone who knew how to turn a phrase.

He grinned back. "No, sir."

The storekeeper put a hand on his heart. "And neither has anyone else. Things were in an uproar at my house. Simon's too, I'm sure."

Jesse eyed him. "Am I causing you trouble?"

"No, no." Mr. James puffed out a sigh. "We are delighted to help, Jesse."

"Is there something I should be doing?" Jesse pressed.

He laughed. "Leave it to the ladies. They've done this a few times now. If they need us, they'll let us know."

It was the same at the restaurant.

"Only one item on the menu tonight," Zeke told him. The lad had been helping Ciara, particularly the last few days when his sister was on her honeymoon. "Ciara's busy cooking for someone's wedding." He nudged Jesse with his shoulder.

"Anything I can do to help?" Jesse asked.

Zeke glanced toward the opening between the dining room and the kitchen. "If I were you, I'd keep out of the way."

So, he kept out of the way. They wouldn't even let him have dinner with Alice. She had no sooner stepped into the restaurant than Ciara popped out of the kitchen and swept her off.

"No seeing the bride this close to the wedding," she scolded Jesse.

So, he ended up arriving at the chapel an hour before the service, dressed in his good clothes, chin freshly shaved, hair neatly combed. Even then he was advised to wait as Mrs. Callie practiced on the organ in one corner near the altar and Mrs. Dottie finished placing vases of holly about.

Finally, Mr. Levi arrived and went to the altar, and guests began filling the pews on either side of the center aisle. Several cast him either commiserating or curious looks.

Kit took pity on him.

"It's a simple ceremony," he assured him, taking Jesse's arm as if he were infirm. "No one's walking anyone down the aisle. Let's get you set up."

Kit positioned him on one side of the minister, then took his place on Jesse's left as they looked toward the door.

Voices went silent. A pew creaked. Something flapped in the rafters.

Mrs. Callie began playing.

Ciara walked up the aisle, smiling. She winked at him before going to take a spot beyond Levi. She trained her gaze down the aisle, and he looked to find Alice standing at the foot.

She was wearing that blue gown with the white swirls again, and she glided toward him like sunlight on a river. White roses made a crown on her dark hair, and a lace veil fell to her shoulders. Light sparkled around her, life, joy.

Jesse couldn't help staring.

Levi smiled as she came up to stand beside him. "Dearly beloved, we are gathered here today," he began.

Jesse had heard the words spoken over Kit and Harry and their brides. They washed over him now as if from a distance. He couldn't take his eyes off Alice. He saw when she dropped her gaze to pray, dark lashes fanning her cheeks inside the lace of the veil. He saw her gown swell when she took a deep breath. He heard her repeat the vows in her calm, sweet voice.

And he took her hand and promised to love and cherish her all the days of his life.

She says not love, God, but You know what the future holds. No matter those words, You know that I will honor her and You.

Mr. Levi finished the ceremony and smiled at them both. Jesse knew what came next, and, by the color climbing in Alice's cheeks, so did she. Carefully, he peeled back the veil from her face. Her eyes were wide and so, so deep.

He bent and brushed his lips against her cheek. Friends could do that, couldn't they?

Friends wouldn't feel so shaken by the touch.

Her smile looked wobbly as he withdrew, but he tucked her hand in his arm and turned to face the others. Every Wallin beamed back, more than one looking misty-eyed. Katie Jo clapped her hands together. Harry clasped his hands over his head in a clear sign of victory.

What therefore God hath joined together, let not man put asunder.

Mr. Levi had said that verse over them, but Jesse heard it ringing in his ears as he led his bride to their reception and into their new life together.

CHAPTER EIGHT

HER WEDDING HAD been lovely, thanks to Ciara and all the other dear ladies of Wallin Landing. Everyone was kind and so very happy for her. It was easy to be as happy. But the most surprising thing about her wedding and reception was how nice it felt being held in Jesse's arms, even on the dancefloor. She was weightless, as if she danced on air. And nothing, and no one, could touch her, not with such a man beside her.

Jesse showed no interest in leaving the hall early, to the point at which several of their guests started giving them the eye. Rina began tidying up the serving dishes on the table. Even Mr. Simon lowered his bow and took a long swig of water as if they had worn him out by playing.

"We should probably be going," she murmured to Jesse as they left the dancefloor after a particularly energetic reel.

He glanced around as well, then gave her a smile. "Sounds good."

She looked to Catherine, who looked to Rina.

"Attention!" she said in her best schoolteacher voice, and the room quieted, bodies stilled. "Our happy couple is ready to start their new life. Let's send them off in style."

Applause thundered. Mr. James put his fingers in his mouth and blew a long whistle. Kit and Harry cheered.

Ciara waved, and Katie Jo rushed forward and enveloped Alice in a hug that nearly crushed the breath from her lungs.

Then her friend stepped back, eyes tearing, and Alice left the hall on Jesse's arm.

He led her down the hill into the main clearing. She turned toward the inn and nearly collided with him.

She stopped on the well-worn path. "Where are we going?"

He hung his head. "Never did find anywhere else to bunk, so I suppose we're going to the school."

The lovely spiced cider Ciara had poured for everyone bubbled in her stomach. "There isn't room for two. I told you that."

"I can sleep on the floor," he volunteered. "Or I could go back to the cabin with Zeke."

He sounded so sad that she didn't have the heart to send him away. Besides, what would people think if she threw out her husband on their wedding night! Gladys Volland was looking for any excuse to let her go.

"We'll make do," she told him, starting forward again. Together, they crossed the clearing for the school.

Alice led him into her quarters. The room off the back of the main schoolroom had originally held a bed, a chest for her things, and a small table and chair by the window looking out at the forest. She had added the trunk she'd sent ahead. Now the other chest Catherine and her sisters-in-law had filled was pressed against the far wall, leaving only a little space at the foot of Alice's bed.

And everything felt much closer with Jesse there too.

He nodded to the patch of floor. "That would do nicely. I'll fetch my quilt and shaving gear from the cabin." He strode back out.

And Alice could breathe.

She peered at the spot, which seemed far too small for his frame, then shook her head. She might have a marriage of convenience, but that didn't mean she couldn't help care for her husband. They would be friends, after all. He'd agreed to that. She started gathering items.

By the time he returned, with a surprisingly small number of belongings, she had put together a credible nest, with a pillow, the extra blankets she had been given for the winter months, and a quilt she'd discovered in Catherine's chest. Somehow she doubted the nurse had known the use to which it would be put.

He smiled at her handiwork. "That looks real cozy. Thank you."

Alice returned his smile. "Anything for my husband."

As soon as she said the words, she regretted them. She'd made it quite clear she was not willing to do some of the things a wife might be expected to do for her husband. But he didn't seem to take offense. He set his razor, soap, and mug on the windowsill, laid his flannel shirt and trousers on the chair, then tucked the rest of his clothes into the chest, careful of her dresses.

A tidy person. What a pleasant surprise.

The room was darkening. The sun had faded beyond the hill behind the school. Alice closed the chintz curtains against the last of its rays, then went to light the lamp on the table. He stood next to the table, shifting from foot to foot and setting the floor boards to creaking.

"Usually go to bed early," he said. "Have to work in the morning."

"Yes, so do I." She licked her lips. "But there is a matter of changing."

"Oh." He straightened to an impressive height. "I'll wait in the school." He strode out the door and shut it behind him.

Well!

Alice's fingers trembled as she worked the buttons on her dress. Her family had never been wealthy enough to employ a lady's maid, as the Cawthorns did. She and her mother had helped each other. At Boston Normal, she and the other students had partnered when needed. Knowing she would have no such help when she traveled West, she'd chosen her clothing with care, thankful for the front-lacing stays that had been all the rage before she'd left.

Still, she undressed and pulled on her nightgown faster than she ever had before. She stowed away her things, climbed into bed, and pulled up the covers before calling, "You may come in now."

He might have been expecting a wolf in the room the way he poked in his head before slowly entering. She pulled the covers even higher, up over her head, and squeezed shut her eyes to give him as much privacy as possible.

Her imagination had no trouble filling the darkness. The rustle of cloth as his coat came off. The snap of a suspender as he must have pulled it free from his broad shoulders. The soft thud of material falling, then the pad of his foot as he dealt with his clothing. A whoosh as he put out the lamp. Finally, a breathy sigh as he must have stretched out.

"Are you comfortable?" she asked.

More rustling. "It's not bad."

That didn't mean it was good. "Is there anything I can do?"

A hesitation that seemed to fill her senses, fill the room.

"No, ma'am, that is, Alice. I'll be fine."

She opened her eyes and lowered the covers from her face. Cool evening air brushed her skin and black pressed against her eyes. Funny. Back home, gas lamps were kept burning even in the residential areas through the night. Here, the only light came from the moon and stars, and when the clouds were out, as they were tonight, there was precious little of that. She and Jesse were wrapped in a cocoon of darkness.

Perhaps that was why it was easier to talk.

"I truly appreciate your understanding about this whole affair," she said. "I know it's a bit unconventional."

"Happy to help."

Alice smiled in the darkness. "I've noticed that about you. You like to help people."

"My parents always said that was why we were put on this earth, to help others."

"Love God and love thy neighbor," Alice agreed. "It is rare to find a person who excels at both."

"Is it? Seems to me Drew Wallin and his family all do. That's one of the reasons I like working for him."

Alice settled deeper into the bed. "Do you like chopping down trees?"

"We don't just chop down trees." His voice was a rumble, and the boards creaked again as he must have shifted. "We find spars for sailing ships so they can travel the world bringing folks things they need. We haul timber to build homes and the furniture that goes in them. On occasion, we even bring fuel for the fire to heat those homes."

She had never thought of the simple skill as so impactful, or Jesse Willets as such a poet.

Who was this man she'd married?

Why was he prosing on about the joys of logging? She could hardly care about the camaraderie built among men doing dangerous work in sometimes challenging conditions.

"It sounds like an important profession," she said as if she did understand. "What do you do in the winter? I imagine you can't work in the elements all year long."

"Most days you can," he allowed. "About the only time we stay out of the woods is when the wind's blowing. The Wallins lost their Pa to a widow maker."

The bed rattled as she must have turned. "What's a widow maker?"

"Dead branch, higher than a man's head. When it comes down, it can break limbs or hit hard enough to kill."

Again the rattle.

"Sorry," Jesse murmured. "Didn't mean to give you a chill."

She was quiet a moment. "How did you know I had a chill?"

"Heard the bed."

"Oh."

The word was small enough, and said in a small enough voice, that he knew he'd embarrassed her.

"What about you?" he asked, turning the subject. "Do you like being a teacher?"

He was fairly sure of the answer. He'd seen the kind way she dealt with her little students and the way they gazed up at her with worshipful eyes.

"Yes," she said. "They are so eager to learn, so excited by every new fact. It makes me see the world through their eyes, and it's beautiful."

Jesse smiled. "My little sisters and brothers were the same way. You might see a sunset a hundred times, but the first time they see the sky painted all red and purple, and their faces light up with awe, you remember how special it is."

"That's it entirely, the awe, the wonder. I hope they never lose it. I hope *I* never lose it again."

Jesse stretched out on the floor. The night air nipped his stockinged feet, warning him that he'd pulled the blanket up too high. It wasn't easy finding one long enough for him, though the one Mrs. Catherine had given him, made by the original Mrs. Wallin, was certainly close. Then again, Ma Wallin had had four strapping sons, so she'd likely known the size needed.

"Why would you lose the wonder?" he asked, curling up into the warmth again.

For a moment, he thought she'd fallen asleep. Then her voice came out soft and a little sad. "I had a disappointment that made me question myself."

He didn't even know what that disappointment was yet, and already he wanted to smash it. "What happened?"

"The man I was supposed to marry decided to marry someone else."

All sleepiness fled. "You were engaged to be married?" *Well, of course, Jesse. Did you think someone as pretty and smart as Alice Dennison just appeared at Wallin Landing with no other fellow noticing along the way?*

"To Roland Cawthorn." He could take some satisfaction in the way she spat out the name. "My parents were beyond delighted. He was the richest, most handsome, most cultured bachelor for miles, you see. Every girl was setting her cap at him. My family and friends all told me how fortunate I was that he would take an interest in me."

Rich. Handsome. Cultured. Was that what she'd hoped for in a husband? He felt smaller by the moment.

"Why'd he call it off?" he made himself ask.

"He said I was too pliable."

Pliable. His Alice. Who could scold a schoolboard president with words having multiple syllables. Who'd stood her ground about their marriage of convenience.

"He didn't know you very well, did he?" he said.

"He should have," she answered tartly. "We courted for two years and were betrothed for one interminable year. He had plenty of time to become better acquainted. I certainly had enough time to convince myself he loved me. But I never could get him to agree on a wedding date. That's one of the reasons I attended Boston Normal."

"He wanted you to go to college?" Jesse asked.

"Very likely not. But I had wanted to go since graduating

from finishing school. When Roland first showed interest, Mother insisted I remain available in town to court. But the hints she and his mother were dropping about setting the date didn't work, so she agreed to allow me to attend. Absence makes the heart grow fonder and all that. Only it didn't seem to make his heart grow in the slightest. He announced he'd decided on another woman to wed."

Jesse snorted. "The more fool him."

He could almost hear the smile in her voice, though it quickly faded. "Thank you, Jesse. But I fear everyone else thought the more fool *me*. There was surely something terribly wrong with me that Roland Cawthorn would risk the scandal of jilting me just to be rid of me."

"I hope they scolded him too," Jesse said, thinking of Mrs. Volland's statement about men not having to worry about their reputation as much as women.

"Oh, his parents might have protested. I think my brother, Gerald, attempted to reason with him. But Roland was certain he'd be happier with Miss Holladay. She was related to Mr. Ben Holladay, who owns the stages and ships. She had something I didn't—money."

Miss Holladay might have had money, but Jesse would never believe she was prettier or sweeter than Alice. "So, you headed West."

"Yes. I decided to start over somewhere new. I saw the advertisement for the Lake Union School. It was circulated at Boston Normal. My teachers were kind enough to recommend me, and the Wallins hired me."

He knew the last part. Mrs. Rina had been so proud of hiring another graduate from that prestigious teachers' college. But Alice shouldn't have felt compelled to take the Wallins' offer just to escape her tormentors. The injustice of her treatment burned like wildfire inside him.

"You were right to come West," he told her. "Those folks didn't appreciate you. Everyone at Wallin Landing can see you're a pearl beyond price."

"Thank you," she murmured again, and it sounded a little watery, like when his sisters had finished a crying bout. His anger only kindled further. Shame on those who had claimed to love her for not supporting her. Shame on Cawthorn for leading her on.

And shame on Jesse if he ever let her down like that.

They fell silent then, and finally sleep overtook him. Still, he woke before dawn as was his habit. He had laid his work clothes on the chair, so he managed to find them and pull them on in the darkness without waking her. Then he carried his boots into the schoolroom to don them.

The woodbox looked a little low, so he went out as the sun was just peaking over the mountains and chopped some wood, brought it into the school, and kindled the fire for her. Across the clearing, Mr. Drew, Kit, and Harry were gathering in front of the inn.

He cracked the door of her quarters open in time to see sunlight anointing her. It turned her cheeks rosy, set a glow to her dark hair. It brushed her pretty lips the way a husband would.

The way he never could.

As if she knew he was watching, she opened her eyes. Pain pierced him at the thought of leaving, worse than cutting himself with a saw.

He shook himself. "Going to work now. Fire's started. See you at dinner."

And every moment until then.

CHAPTER NINE

SUCH A TENDER look. Alice lay for a moment after Jesse had gone, savoring it. She might have thought she was made of fine crystal or shining gold, precious and beautiful. What a lovely way to start the morning!

So was the fire. She'd dressed for the day in her purple lustring with the bow at the waist, then swathed herself in the canvas apron Ciara had loaned her to go to battle with the hearth. But when she stepped into the schoolroom, she found the fire crackling merrily and the space warm and cozy. She could get used to that too!

Perhaps it was Jesse's smile, perhaps the warm room, but the school day went even better than usual. Lars seemed to have decided to embrace his new role, for he helped Anna sound out her letters and grinned at her when she mastered her sums for the day. The other children focused on their spelling and arithmetic as well.

Even better was their excursion. She had arranged for Mr. John to give the children a tour of the Wallin Landing Library. Alice had always loved libraries, from the Cawthorn Reading Room in the little white house near the church to the high-ceilinged room with the tall windows that had housed the library at Boston Normal. She'd even envied Roland the massive family library in his parents' grand mansion, though she had to wonder now how many of the gilt-edged tomes he had bothered to read. Perhaps, like Roland's devotion, they had been all for show.

The Wallin Landing Library was a simple log cabin near the park that ran along the shores of Lake Union. She had to stop David from throwing rocks into the blue-gray waters as they passed, and even John Bradshaw eyed the shallows with interest.

But the library held so many more treasures! Just stepping through the green door and inhaling the heady mix of cedar and leather brought a smile to her face. Light from the windows on opposite sides of the little cabin fell on bookshelves filled to the groaning point. Alice's fingers itched to peruse the offerings.

Mr. John rose from his place at a desk in the center of the riches and smiled at her students.

"Welcome to the Wallin Landing Library," he told them as they huddled a little closer to Alice as if aware of the honor.

"Do you really own all these books, Uncle John?" David asked in an awed voice, glancing around.

He chuckled. "No, Davy. You do. You all do."

Her students stared at him.

"The library belongs to everyone in Wallin Landing," he explained. "Each person can take home one book at a time. If they bring it back in good shape, they can choose another."

Mavis raised her hand, and Alice nodded her permission to speak, glad the girl was improving at the practice.

"Do you have any books about princesses?" she asked Mr. John.

He rubbed his chin. "I believe we do, but they might be a little difficult for you to read right now."

"I'm eight," she informed him haughtily. "I'm a very good reader."

"Perhaps we could pick a book for the classroom we

can all enjoy," Alice suggested. "I'll read a little aloud to you after lunch each day, if we finish our morning assignments."

This seemed agreeable to all, and in the end they decided on *Around the World in Eighty Days* by Mr. Jules Verne. And each of the children except Mavis, whose nose was still out of joint—she held a grudge as well as her mother!—took a book home to read as well.

"I could wipe off the chalkboard if you like, Miss D—that is Mrs. Willets," John Bradshaw offered, broad cheeks turning red, as they ended the school day in the classroom.

"Someone likes the teacher," Mavis teased, sashaying past on her way to the door.

"*Everyone* likes the teacher," Lars corrected her with a frown.

"That would be very kind of you, John," Alice told him. "Perhaps we can start a rotation. Whoever gets the most questions right that day may clean off the board."

The others exchanged eager grins before following Mavis out the door.

John had the board cleaned in no time, stepping back to admire his handiwork with a nod.

"Very nice," Alice told him, putting away the last of the chalk. "Thank you, John."

"You're welcome." He turned and met her gaze. "I wish you'd married my pa instead." Then, head down, he fled.

Alice sighed. She wasn't sure how to explain to the boy that she'd made the best choice for them both.

The door opened, and James came loping in. He wove his way between the desks to hold out an envelope to her. "I was getting bored at the store, so I thought I'd deliver the mail. This came for you."

It took everything in her to keep her smile pleasant and reach for the letter. "Thank you."

He cocked his head, blue eyes sparkling with curiosity. "Family?"

"Very likely," she said, though her heart started beating faster. "Rina should be done. I'm sure she'd love to see you."

He winked at her. "You read my mind." He sauntered out the door for the other classroom.

Alice set the letter on her desk. She could feel it there, glowering, as she brushed off the desks and swept the floor. The fire was low. She eyed it a moment before going to lay a log gingerly on top, yanking back her hands as it spit and sizzled.

There was coal just on the other side of Lake Washington. Surely someone could spare a few pieces for a stove instead of a hearth in the school, particularly for the room holding the littler children. It was for safety as well as convenience. Perhaps she should suggest the investment to the schoolboard.

The thought of the board reminded her of Mrs. Volland's animosity, and that made her look at the letter on her desk again.

Was she a schoolmarm or wasn't she? She had no reason to fear a little letter!

She marched up to her desk and seized the thing, then ripped open one end.

Dear daughter.

Ah, from her parents then. And there was her mother's signature at the bottom. What, had she thought Roland would actually deign to write to her?

We continue to be concerned about your precipitous departure.

She wasn't the only one who multiplied her syllables when stressed.

It was quite unlike your usual, thoughtful approach to life's challenges.

Yes, for once, she had chosen to take matters into her

own hands rather than to allow others to dictate her future. Shocking.

And your refusal to respond to our telegrams indicates that you are no easier in your mind.

No, her refusal to respond to their demands that she return home at once indicated her confidence that she was right where she should be. That, and a need to economize. She hadn't her parents', or Roland's, income to rely on.

Everyone here is so worried for you. You had no reason to run off like that.

Being thrown over on the flimsiest of excuses after waiting years? Being ridiculed and berated by family and so-called friends? They seemed viable reasons to her.

Please, come home. All is forgiven.

She had no expectation that all had been forgiven or forgotten. If she went home, women would whisper at society events about how sad it was such a nice girl was a spinster. Men would wonder at her flaws that Roland Cawthorn would throw her over. Every time she went to church, someone would point out that she could be the woman sitting in the elaborate front pew reserved for the Cawthorn family.

So, how to answer her mother? A smile curved her mouth. Why, she could mimic her new husband and respond as Jesse would.

No.

She sighed as she set down the letter. However satisfying in the moment that would be, she would feel guilty afterward for so terse a response. Just because her parents couldn't understand her side of the issue didn't mean she didn't understand theirs.

Her father was the head of accounting for Cawthorn Industries. His family had existed on the edges of Cawthorn upper society for generations. He'd been proud enough that Gerald and Roland had formed a friendship in school. To have the premiere family accept his daughter as the wife of their son would have elevated him and her mother into rare air indeed. How could she have ruined such an opportunity for them?

She had come to the realization that she must build her life in a different way, in a different place. Where Roland had left her in darkness, God had given her a place of light. She would not allow her parents to pull her back into the dark.

She took a sheet of paper and began writing.

Dear Mother and Father, I haven't had an opportunity to write before, in part because my duties as schoolteacher here in Wallin Landing keep me so busy.

They couldn't understand the hurt and anger that had been the larger reason not to write beyond letting them know she had arrived safely, so there was no reason to belabor the point.

I have eight students in my class, and each one is bright and enthusiastic. It is a joy to teach them.

That much was completely true. Every day when she looked out on the eager faces she knew herself blessed.

There is no need for me to return to Cawthorn. I am content here, and I recently married a fine, upstanding man you would admire.

She stopped and sucked in a breath. No, her parents would not admire Jesse. He had neither the wealth nor the family connections, which is what made a man in their view. They would not see his kind nature, the willingness to help others, that she found so commendable.

She pulled out another sheet and copied the first few lines, then continued.

I am content here, and I recently married a fine, upstanding man that I much admire. Give my love to Gerald. Your daughter, Alice.

"Jesse!"

He shook himself and pulled his ax out of the tree. "Sorry!"

They had been working to the north of the settlement, along the edge of the hill, bringing down a few choice cedar needed to build furniture in Seattle, but Drew had pointed them to a stand of nearby fir today. Something about logs for a new cabin someone was building. Jesse was supposed to be felling this particular tree. Instead, he'd caught himself thinking about Alice, lying there with the sun on her lips, and his work had disappeared in fog.

"Second time today," Drew told him, coming around the tree from where he'd been preparing another. "I can guess where your mind is. You should be on your honeymoon."

Harry and Kit, who had begun to saw the long blade through one of the larger trees, stopped their work to look his way too. His cheeks heated, and he knew it wasn't from the sunlight streaming through the branches.

"Alice is needed to teach," he said. "And I need to work. We can take a honeymoon trip later."

"Catherine and I waited until Hans was five before we took ours," his employer said, resting his ax head on the needle-strewn ground and leaning on the handle. "But Levi and Beth were still in the cabin, so we didn't want to take the time."

Drew was the oldest of the Wallin siblings, and Jesse had heard the story of how he had stepped in at only eighteen years of age to raise his brothers and sister after their father had been killed. He would have done the same for his little brothers and sisters, but he was beyond thankful that nothing had happened to his father.

"Which means you don't have an excuse, Jesse," Harry called. "The Occidental Hotel in Seattle is a fine place."

It was indeed. Perhaps even fine enough for his beautiful

bride. Did friends take friends to a hotel for a few days? They'd had a good talk last night, but it was one of the first. Two days in Seattle, alone.

Talking.

Jesse shuddered.

"Anything would be better than sleeping in the schoolmarm's room," Harry reminded him as if he'd seen his reaction. Of course they all knew he was staying with Alice. They just didn't know he was sleeping on the floor.

"He won't be doing that for long," Drew said. He nodded to Jesse. "There's a reason we're felling fir today. We're throwing you a house raising tomorrow. Every Wallin brother and his wife, Harry and Katie Jo, Kit and Ciara, Zeke McCallister, Hitchcock, Bradshaw, and Volland have all agreed to pitch in."

Jesse's ax fell to the ground with a thud. "But there's a lot of work left to do."

Drew laughed. "That's an understatement, but many hands make light work. We'll have that cabin done before sundown."

Jesse swallowed. They might have finished the original cabin that fast, but not the one he needed now.

"We may have to alter it a bit," he confessed. "I decided I want two sleeping rooms."

"Then you better start cutting more trees," Drew teased him with a chuckle.

They were all grinning now, and he was pretty sure why. They thought he wanted the extra room for the children he and Alice would have.

And he couldn't tell them that the extra room would be for him.

Alice had just finished her letter to her parents when Jesse burst through the schoolroom door. His eyes were wide, his russet hair was going every which way, and his breath came fast, as if he'd run from wherever they'd been working in the forest.

She surged to her feet. "Jesse, what's wrong?"

"They want to build us a house," he said.

She caught her breath. For a moment, she'd feared he'd been hurt, and every part of her had tightened. "What?"

"Mr. Drew and the others," he elaborated, jogging toward her. "They want to finish the cabin for us."

Alice blinked. "Why, how kind." She slipped the letter into the envelope and sealed it. "When will they start work?"

"Tomorrow," Jesse said. "They aim to have it finished by sunset."

She stared at him. "Sunset, tomorrow?"

He nodded.

Alice collapsed back against the chair. "Oh, my."

He nodded again. "Exactly."

Alice straightened. "Well, we need to be ready, then." She pulled a piece of paper closer. "What remains to be accomplished?"

"Floor," he said, pacing about the room. "Door. Furnishings. Overhang on the porch if we want such. And I asked them to add a second sleeping room. Because, you know."

Alice had been making a list. Now she looked up, stomach sinking. "You told them?"

He frowned. "No. They think I want the room for all the children we'll have."

Was there a hitch in his voice? Perhaps he was merely as shaken as she was by such generosity.

"Well, that's fine, then," she said, attempting to focus on the list again. "Will we need paint for the interior? Rugs for the floor? Catherine and the other ladies filled a chest for us with dishes, linens, and the like. And what about a stove?"

He grimaced. "Interior is log, so no paint for now.

Maybe we can make a rug this winter. Can't afford a stove for cooking just yet, and likely we'd have to wait for one to be brought from San Francisco. We can cook in the hearth and save up."

She glanced at the fire, which was slowly dying. "You might have noticed I have some trouble with hearths."

"I'll teach you," he said. "Or I can do the cooking."

She sagged. "You truly are a kind-hearted soul, Jesse. Thank you. But you shouldn't have to do everything. I promise to watch you and learn. Now, what else must be done?"

It was less of a challenge than usual to get her husband to tell her his thoughts. Perhaps it was because he knew his plan for the cabin well. Perhaps he merely wanted to make the best use of this opportunity. Either way, she had a good list by the time they went to dinner at the inn.

They settled at one of the smaller tables. Zeke came to take their orders.

"Bet you're going to like having your meals at home soon," he joked to Jesse.

Jesse just smiled.

Bless him. Theirs was not the marriage either of them had likely intended, but he was trying to make the best of it. And so would she.

That's why she took her list to Ciara in the kitchen. Her friend had come West from New York as a girl. She'd help build the old Wallin family cabin into this inn and helped Kit with their own cabin. She'd know if Alice and Jesse had missed anything.

Ciara perused the list as she stood over her cooking. Wallin Landing might be a small settlement, but the black and silver stove was better than many that graced a Cawthorn home. Alice could only wonder how long it had taken to bring the thing all the way to Seattle.

Pork and cider stew was on the menu that night, and the savory scents drifted through the doorway into the restaurant, where a dozen eager customers were already giving their orders to Zeke and Katie Jo, who was back from her honeymoon.

"Kit and Drew talked to me about their plans for tomorrow," Ciara told Alice. "A dozen men and nearly that many women, most of whom know their way around a saw and a hammer. They should be able to get through your list, but we should feed them."

Once more, Alice's stomach sank. "I don't think I can manage that."

Ciara rested the ladle against the side of the stew and gave Alice's hand a squeeze. "You don't have to. We're all doing this for you and Jesse. I made a couple of pots of potato soup this afternoon that will keep until tomorrow and four dozen biscuits. With jugs of cider and plenty of water, we should be able to get them through the day. By this time tomorrow night, you could be moving into your own home."

CHAPTER TEN

AFTER TALKING WITH her friend, Alice was feeling far more in control of the situation as she and Jesse walked back to the schoolroom following dinner.

"Where exactly is your cabin?" she asked. Somewhere in the woods an owl called, and she spotted James taking his horses to the barn from the pasture.

"Bit to the north," he told her, "though near enough that you can walk to school."

A wall of trees marked the northern boundary of the settlement. "You have a claim so close?"

"Yes."

Alice smiled to herself as they reached the door of the school. "A bit more elaboration, please, Jesse. I understood homestead claims were one hundred and sixty acres. That seems farther than I'd be able to walk to school, particularly in the winter."

He held the door open for her. "The claims are closer together here than usual. When the Wallin family settled the area, their pa wanted to start his own town. So, he and Ma Wallin took narrow claims side by side, running from the lake to the top of the hill. Claims for Drew, James, and John lay to the south, Simon's to the north, and his wife, Nora took a claim that runs along the top of the hill, tying them together."

Alice put out her lower lip as he shut the door. They'd

left a single lamp burning, so most of the schoolroom was in shadow. "I didn't know women could file claims."

"Not sure I ever heard of an unmarried lady filing a claim," he admitted, "but I never heard they couldn't. Every woman I know who filed a claim was the wife of another claim holder. That's how my ma and pa had enough land for the ranch."

As if he'd worn out his allotted number of words for the day, he went to bank the fire for the night. And he stayed in the schoolroom again until Alice had changed and was safely abed.

"We won't have to do this when we have our own home," she told him as he climbed into his nest of covers on the floor in the dark. "And you can have your own bed."

He grunted, which she took as agreement. Then he settled into his bed with no more than a "Night, Alice."

Just as well. Her mind was still too full of plans to talk about anything else. She was surprised she fell asleep so quickly.

On Saturday, she wore her most practical gown—a blue and white striped cotton with only one overskirt trimmed in ruffles—put Ciara's canvas apron on top and gathered her list, three pencils, and additional paper. Ciara had oatmeal with raisins and honey ready for breakfast. Alice could only hope it would be enough to fuel those who were coming to work.

"Go on," Ciara urged her when Alice offered to help wash dishes. "You'll want to be there when they arrive. I'll be right behind you."

Jesse walked her to the northwest corner of the clearing, near the big trees with the children's swings. She didn't see a path until he lifted a heavy fir bough out of the way. Then she spotted the shadowed route.

"Suppose I better cut that," he said as he let the bough fall behind her. "Might not always be with you."

"Very thoughtful of you," Alice said.

The path was wide enough that they could go side by side, past bushes and plants she was beginning to know. Dusky-leafed rhododendron, which she had been told would bloom with white multi-flowered blossoms in the spring. Lacy-leafed red huckleberry, the tart fruit mostly gone now for the year. Broad-leafed bracken and towering fir and cedar. She inhaled the cool, moist air.

Something brushed her fingers, and Jesse's hand slipped around hers.

Warmth flowed.

"In case you stumble," he hurriedly assured her.

"Very kind," Alice replied, but she walked a little closer anyway.

He had been right, she saw. They hadn't strolled more than a few minutes before the woods opened up to another clearing, much smaller. Sunlight speared down to brighten the cedar shake roof of a little two-room cabin. A porch extended from a boarded up opening she assumed would be the front door, with a real glass-paned window on either side of that opening. The chimney was made of rounded stones in white, gray, and tan, like the lakeshore bound vertically.

"It's lovely," she said.

He pinked. "Harry helped me put in a pump, right outside the back door, so you won't have to go to the lake or the crick for water. And Kit helped me put in that chimney." He nodded to one side, where a pile of logs and cut boards lay waiting. "And they brought out the timber for the flooring and the second bedroom."

"You've done stellar work," she told him. "That is, excellent work."

He gave her a look but didn't respond.

"Greetings to the house!"

James and Rina came along the path, a wooden crate of tools in his arms. Rina's arms were filled with fabric.

"Curtains for the windows," she told Alice as they drew closer. "Courtesy of Nora. She's watching the little ones today so the rest of us can work. Your students complained, but I promised them you'd give them a tour when we were finished."

Much as she loved her boys and girls, they would likely have been underfoot today. And they might not have been safe with so many saws and hammers going.

And those tools and many others went into action fast. John and Levi took on the flooring, the sound of their mallets a counterpoint to the rasp of the saws Mr. Hitchcock and Mr. Bradshaw were using to cut the timber for the door. Simon and James were up on the roof, planning where to set the overhang for the porch as well as how to build out the roof to cover the second room. Katie Jo and Zeke were preparing the ground to the east of the cabin for the other room, clearing away brush, leveling the area, and bringing stones for the foundation. Jesse, Drew, and Harry were planing off the bark and squaring up the logs for the room, while Mr. Volland cut notches in the ends.

That was the only fly in the ointment. Mr. Volland had brought his wife.

Mrs. Volland had been helping Rina hang the curtains, but she came out onto the porch to look at everyone's handiwork, arms akimbo, as if preparing to critique. Instead, she latched onto Alice as she passed with a bucket full of mortar she, Catherine, and Dottie had been mixing to chink the logs.

"This is a great deal of bother, Mrs. Willets," she said. "You might have saved us all the trouble if you and your husband had gone home to your family as they advised."

Alice stepped away from her, nearly dropping the bucket in the process. "How do you know my family advised me to leave?"

The saws ground to a halt as Mr. Hitchcock and Mr. Bradshaw looked at her askance as well.

"What have you put your nose in now, Gladys?" her husband asked with a sigh, resting his ax on the ground.

"I'm sure I don't know what you're talking about," she said, but her gaze darted around like that of a cornered mouse. "It is well known that Mrs. Willets attended Boston Normal. Therefore, she came from that area. Therefore, she has a family who is no doubt missing her. I merely suggested that she might wish to see them again."

"No," Alice said with a look to her husband. "I don't. Thank you for asking. Now, if you'll excuse me, I have a house to build."

That look. Part independence and part pride, and for him alone. A man could get used to that.

It was a little hard to get used to this much help, though. He was generally the one folks called on for help, so to find his friends gathered on his behalf was a little unnerving. And they all seemed to have questions.

"What color do you want the door?" the blacksmith asked, rattling the iron latch he'd brought with him. "We might as well paint it before we put on the other pieces."

"Blue," Alice said, passing with a bucket of water and cups for the workers.

"Blue," Jesse said with a smile. "That sounds nice."

"Where do you want us to put the window for the bedroom?" Harry asked, wiping sweat from his brow with the back of one hand. The sun had stayed out all day, as if offering a blessing to their work.

"Front?" Jesse mused.

"East," Alice said, bringing John and Levi another cask of nails for the floor. "So we'll get the morning sun."

"And know when to wake up," Jesse said. "Smart."

"East it is," Harry said. "Though I'm not sure I'd want to get out of bed so early." He winked at Jesse.

They took a break at midday for the food Ciara had brought, then went right back at it. He was used to working all day, yet even his muscles were starting to protest. He wasn't sure how, except that Alice kept them all on task, but as the sun started slanting through the trees, they finished the cabin. They'd had to lever the last few upper logs into place on the second room, and it had taken five of them to put the shake roof over it. But it stood level and true, with curtains at the window, the glass for which James Wallin had had Zeke bring up from the mercantile.

"But don't lean against it for a few days," he'd advised Jesse as Drew and Harry had put it into place. "It will take a while for that mortar to set up."

Now Drew stood in front of the house, one arm about Catherine. "I'd be proud to bring my wife home to that."

Jesse slipped his arm around Alice's waist. "Me too."

He thought she might pull away, but she beamed at him. "Our home."

Something swelled in his heart. He decided to think of it as pride, for now.

The only things that hadn't been finished were the furnishings. Ciara had donated one of the smaller tables from the restaurant, and Simon had provided two chairs for it. Rina had told Alice to take her bed and things from the schoolhouse, but Jesse knew he'd have to build a second bed, long enough for him to stretch out. Enough smaller logs were left that he should be able to put together a frame. But, for at least another night or two, they would have to make do with Alice's room.

He'd seen no bathing tub or even space to store it, but he knew he needed to rinse off before he climbed into his bedding. "You go ahead," he told Alice, opening the door of the school for her. "I need to clean up."

She put a hand on his arm. "Where are you going to do that?"

In the summer, he might have jumped in the lake, but not tonight. Shadows were creeping across the clearing. Along with them came the chill of an autumn evening.

Jesse ran a hand back through his hair. "Not sure."

"You start the fire," Alice said. "Leave the rest to me."

By the time he had the fire kindled, she brought him a teakettle and tucked it into the coals.

"It will take a bit for that to heat," she said, straightening. "Then we can mix it with the cold water, and you can rub down."

Her cheeks turned pink, as if even mentioning him with his shirt off embarrassed her. She'd worked hard that day, pitching in wherever she could. Now dirt and mortar speckled her apron, and something gray streaked her nose.

Jesse reached up and wiped it away with the pad of his thumb. "You might want to rub down too."

Her cheeks only darkened before she turned away.

In the end, they took turns near the fire, Alice first and then Jesse, at his insistence. Then he banked the fire for the night and slipped into the room and his pile of bedding.

"I've been handwashing my things the same way," Alice said. The bedstead creaked as she must have burrowed deeper under the covers. "But I can't do that with yours. Who does the laundry in Wallin Landing?"

Jesse chuckled. "Every lady and single gent who needs it. Seems like Monday is the day, because I see clothes strung up on lines from every cabin."

She was quiet a moment. "Perhaps Ciara can show me how."

Jesse levered himself up on his elbow, but he still couldn't make out more than a darker lump on the bed. "You never washed clothes?"

"My mother paid a local lady." Her voice was small again, as if she had admitted to stealing the ham. "But I'm sure I can learn."

Jesse lay back down. "I know you can. You already proved you could learn enough to be a schoolmarm. Washing clothes will be nothing."

"Thank you, Jesse." Now there was a smile in her voice, which had gained a little volume again. "Mrs. Volland would probably say that not knowing how to wash clothes proves I should have stayed in Cawthorn. As it is, I simply cannot understand why she keeps insisting that I leave."

"She sure has a bee in her bonnet," Jesse agreed.

"For a moment this morning, I thought she might have been reading my mail."

"Mr. James wouldn't allow that," he told her. "And her husband never goes in for the mail from Seattle that I know." Then the meaning of her words sank in. "Did you get a letter from home?"

"Yes." Her voice was smaller again, with an edge of worry. "My parents asked me to come back. I told them I was married."

Jesse shifted on the floor, muscles tightening despite the effort he'd put them to. "I don't think I could live in Boston. I'm already a far piece from my family as it is. But if you wanted to visit, I could find the money for a train ticket."

"No." Now her voice was decidedly prim. "Thank you. I am quite content. Good night, Jesse."

"Night, Alice."

He lay awake for longer than he'd expected, listening as her breath evened out. He thought he could find contentment as her husband. He could only pray she would find contentment as his wife.

Alice made him toast and tea for breakfast the next morning. She was so proud of the charred pieces of bread that he didn't mention the griddle cakes Ciara had promised him. He held the umbrella over them both as they ventured across to the chapel for services. The sunlight of the last few days had melted into a more typical misty drizzle, turning the air raw and setting the trees to glistening. He nodded to Harry and Katie Jo, Kit and Ciara, and the various Wallins before taking a seat with Alice and entering into worship.

One word kept coming to mind.

Thanks.

Perhaps the good Lord thought one word, spoken only in his heart, wasn't enough, because after his sermon, Levi made a point of mentioning the house raising.

"And we have a new cabin in the settlement, I am pleased to say." He looked to Jesse.

Jesse smiled and nodded.

Alice nudged him. "I think he wants you to stand and talk."

Jesse stared at her. Then his gaze jumped to the preacher, who smiled encouragingly. Others were looking his way as well. Even his single word evaporated.

Jesse swallowed, but still nothing came out.

Alice put her hand on his arm and turned her face up to his, sweet, entreating, and her dimples popped into view.

Didn't he call himself a man? Jesse made himself stand tall and nodded all around. "Thanks." He plopped back down into his seat.

Laughter rippled through the church.

Alice rose, graceful, poised. "What my husband wanted to impart," she said, voice carrying throughout the building, "is that we are eternally grateful for the outpouring of support and friendship we have received from this community. Please know that if we can ever return the favor, you have only to call on us."

There was a smattering of applause as she resumed her seat.

"I bet she's a good schoolmarm," someone muttered behind them. "She sure talks nice."

Alice must have heard him too, for she ducked her head.

"Thanks," Jesse said as they exited the church. Then he grimaced. Surely he could find more than one word for his own wife! "That is, thank you for standing up for me. I never know what to say."

"What you said was perfectly fine," she replied, opening the umbrella and lifting it high enough to cover them both. "Some people just seemed to need a little more elaboration."

Ahead, under the closest tree, Drew and Bradshaw were talking. His employer waved them over.

"Seems Mrs. Volland has been complaining," Drew said as the blacksmith nodded a greeting. "Too many Wallins, doing too many of the jobs. She thinks the schoolboard should be making more of the decisions about how the settlement is run."

"But the purpose of the schoolboard is to make decisions for the school," Alice protested. "Surely others can concern themselves with matters beyond the school."

"That's what I told her," the blacksmith said approvingly. "What we really need is a mayor, a town council."

"You mean incorporation." Drew shook his head. "I'm not sure we're ready for that. Seattle tried it in 1865, but they voted it down two years later."

"But they did eventually bring it back," Bradshaw insisted. "And we're more organized than Seattle. What do you think, Willets?"

They all looked to Jesse. In this smaller group, it wasn't hard to answer. "I suppose we should talk about it."

"Excellent idea," Alice said, so enthusiastically he might have managed to gain Washington its statehood. "I propose we schedule a meeting. Surely Mrs. Volland isn't the only one with opinions on the matter."

CHAPTER ELEVEN

ALL IN ALL, Alice was rather pleased with herself as she and Jesse sat with the Wallins that afternoon. She had paid Ciara for lemons and sugar and made lemonade, so she finally had something to contribute to the meal, and she was delighted to see more than one Wallin gentleman smack his lips after taking a sip. Jesse downed two tall glasses.

Though she did wonder whether it was to get the lingering taste of her slightly burned toast out of his mouth.

He might not have been born a gentleman, but he was truly a gentle man. Even the children realized that, coming to tug on his hand and ask him to play drop the handkerchief. He towered over them, even sitting cross-legged on the rough wood floor.

"Will you play, Mrs. Willets?" Lars asked.

Sitting at the long table, she smiled at him and plucked at her dark skirts, the beads catching the light. "I'm not dressed for it, Lars. But thank you so much for asking. You are every inch the gentleman I named you."

He turned red and hurried off.

"You have elevated his stature," Catherine said on her other side. "He wasn't too sure about sitting with Anna Kincaid. Some of the older boys teased him. But you appealed to his kind nature, which won the day."

Now Alice felt her own cheeks heating. "I'm glad he took the assignment to heart. Anna needs someone kind to watch over her."

Catherine's gaze drifted to her husband, across the table from her. "Don't we all?"

Drew, his brothers, and several of their wives were deep in discussion about Mrs. Volland's challenge to settlement leadership. Alice leaned forward to listen.

"But incorporation is a big step," Drew mused.

"Right in line with Father's dream, though," Simon told him.

"The question is, can we manage the finances that go with that?" John put in.

"Can we manage all the *documents* that go with that?" James challenged. "If you thought proving you'd settled your claim was difficult, wait until you see the mountains of proof that the territory likely expects when chartering a new town." He rolled his eyes skyward as if begging heaven for help.

"Alice is quite right," Rina said with a nod of approval in her direction. "This is a discussion for everyone."

"Even Gladys Volland?" her husband teased.

"Especially people like Mrs. Volland," she insisted. "Better to know and meet the objections in the beginning than fall victim to them in the end."

"Then let's call that meeting," Levi said. "Saturday afternoon, when most people have finished their work for the week and school is out. We can hold it here in the hall."

No one protested the idea.

"That's settled, then," Catherine said. "I'll draft a handbill to post at the church, restaurant, store, post office, and library. That way nearly everyone will see one."

"We should post one in the school as well," Alice said, then quickly looked to Rina, who again nodded her approval.

"You sure kicked a hornet's nest," Jesse said as they walked back to the school.

Only for a few more days, Alice hoped.

"I'd say a beehive," she countered as they reached the school. "And I hope these particular bees can be persuaded to produce honey. Just think, Jesse!" She turned and gazed out at the clearing. "A real town, with a mayor and a council. We'll be part of making history!"

He studied the clearing as if giving the matter thought, but she couldn't imagine he could see what she was seeing. If Cawthorn could be founded and run by one family for generations, how much better could the settlement be run by a number of families banding together, unified by hope in the future?

It was a little early to retire, so they settled at the table by the window. Alice had brought in one of the tall stools so they both had a seat. Jesse had picked up a few small green branches somewhere and proceeded to work at one with a short knife that glinted in the light.

First he cut a small notch, then he drew a line with the point of his knife all the way around the branch. She hadn't realized what he was about until the entire end peeled off in one long tube. Next, he set about deepening the notch. He said nothing as he worked, strong hands, sure and patient.

"Would you like me to read to you?" Alice offered.

He glanced up with a smile. "Sure. What have you got?"

"*Around the World in 80 Days*," she said. "By Mr. Jules Verne. I've been reading it to the children."

He wrinkled his nose, making him look a little like a giant rabbit. "Already read it."

He could read? Alice eyed him. "What did you think about Passepartout?"

"He wasn't much of a valet," he said with a shake of his head, bending over his work again. "But he came through in the end when he discovered they were actually ahead by a day."

He truly did read! She dropped her gaze, embarrassed. She should not have assumed that just because he'd been raised in the wilds and preferred not to speak that he hadn't received any schooling. What else didn't she know about her husband?

She propped her chin on her hands. "What's your favorite story?"

"Oh." He blew out a breath and leaned back, setting stick and knife on the table. "That's hard. My mother read us *Alice's Adventures in Wonderland* growing up. That was interesting. But Mr. John introduced me to John Fenimore Cooper and the Leatherstocking Tales."

"*The Last of the Mohicans*!" Alice straightened. "Oh, it was so romantic!"

"Romantic!" He stared at her. "Uncas and Cora both die in the end!"

"But Alice didn't," she said, raising her chin. "She made a perfectly good marriage with Major Heyward."

"She ought to have married the other fellow," he said. "Heyward never struck me as very brave in the face of things. He let Hawkeye and the Mohicans do all the work. And what did Uncas get as thanks? Killed off, his father left grieving."

"Well, yes," she allowed. "That was bad of Mr. Fenimore Cooper. He does seem to favor odd matches."

He turned his gaze out the window, where twilight was tiptoeing closer. "I know odder ones."

Did he mean their own? Some might agree with him. *She* had agreed with him in the beginning. But the more she came to know her husband, the more she appreciated him.

And the more she wondered about whether she'd made a mistake in insisting on a marriage of convenience.

Jesse listened as Alice read from *Around the World in Eighty Days*, which he'd agreed to reread. He wasn't surprised she liked books, only that they liked the same sort of books. They'd swapped favorites until the sun had faded and he'd had to light the lamp, which burned now between them at the little table. It was past time for bed, but he couldn't bring himself to interrupt her.

He was on his fifth whistle now, and it was coming along nicely. He held it up and blew off some shavings.

"You're certainly making a lot of those," she said. "What are they?

"Thought you might wonder." He worked at skimming down the end. "From what I heard at the hall today, some of the boys need encouragement to tend to their studies. I thought if you used willow bark whistles for prizes, they might knuckle down."

He picked up one of the finished pieces and blew through the end. The toot echoed in the quiet.

She lowered the book. "Why, Jesse, that's brilliant."

He liked when she praised him. He just wished she didn't always sound so surprised.

"How many do you need?" he asked.

She cocked her head, sending a black curl to teasing her cheek. "Can you make eight? The girls could use motivation as well."

"I'll have them done by the end of the day tomorrow," he promised.

She watched him a moment, making no move to pick up the book again. Normally, when he caught people watching, he only felt more self-conscious. Something about the way Alice looked at him made him want to do the best, be the best.

"Will it always be this way?" she murmured.

Jesse frowned, slipping the bark back over the hole.

"No. I aim to finish the other bed by Wednesday. We move into our new house next week."

Her smile was soft, and her dimples appeared. "I meant the two of us, together."

"For as long as we both shall live," he said. "That's what Mr. Levi had us promise."

Her smile deepened. "He did indeed. And will you make willow bark whistles for all my students?"

"Any that need them," he allowed.

"Me teaching, you logging," she mused, closing the book as if she had decided enough was enough for one day.

"I didn't intend to stay a logger," he said. "That's why I claimed the land I did." He wasn't sure why he was telling her. Still, didn't wives need to know what was on their husband's minds?

Didn't wives need to be certain their husband *had* a mind?

"A rancher then," she said. "Like your father. Milk cows in particular are much needed, from what I can see. Few people have them, and milk, butter, and cheese are precious. But I would think that would require space to graze them, and there doesn't appear to be a lot of pastureland in this area unless you plan to cut down a great many more trees."

He chuckled. "I'd have to cut down every tree on my claim. Don't plan on doing that anytime soon." He started on the next whistle. "No, I was thinking of something else the area needs. Fruit. I want to plant an apple orchard."

She clasped her hands. "Oh, Jesse. What a worthwhile dream!"

He glanced up. Her eyes were shining, her lips slightly parted as if in wonder. "You really think so?"

"Absolutely," she said with such certainty he could not doubt her. "I'd go so far as to say it is a noble dream. The entire area exists on Nature's bounty, but that fades over the winter. Apples can be stored for months. Dried, they last even longer."

"That's what I thought," he said, laying the whistle aside. "The first Mrs. Wallin brought apple seeds with her on the Oregon Trail and planted them here. Only one took, but it's now a big tree next to the restaurant. I figured if I saved some of the seeds, I could use them come spring to plant my own orchard."

She nodded eagerly. "I know just the spot. That opening to the south of the cabin. Why, it wouldn't take much for you to widen it. We could probably put in six or eight trees. And each year, we can save some of the seeds, and you can widen the clearing, until we have dozens!"

Her excitement was contagious. He could almost see the orchard stretching from the shores of Lake Union to the hillside.

"So, eventually, instead of cutting trees down, I'll be tending them," he said with a grin.

"It sounds perfect," she agreed.

The only thing more perfect was the thought that she'd be tending them with him.

"I'm glad you like the idea of an orchard," he said as they settled into their respective beds a while later. "Ma told us the story of Johnny Appleseed when we were little. I always thought he knew what he was about."

"Jesse Appleseed," she said with a yawn. "I like it."

So did he.

He was still grinning the next morning when he woke in time to lay the fire for her and dash across the clearing to meet Drew and the others.

His employer was eyeing the sky, which was an angry red to the east.

"Red sky at morning, sailor take warning," Kit said, and Jesse thought he heard a rumble in the distance.

"Not sure how much work we'll get done today," Drew agreed. "Let's move."

The next few days, the rain galloped across the area in bands, allowing them just enough time to take down a few more of the cedars needed to fulfill their contract. Life fell into a pattern—rise and set the fire for Alice, grab something for breakfast at the restaurant if he had time, work for Drew all day, and return to the settlement by late afternoon. With what light was left in the day, he managed to craft a bedstead for the other room of the house, long enough for his frame. And if it was wide enough for two, no one could blame him for hoping. Nora sewed him a tick, and Volland sold him enough dry hay to stuff it. Now all that remained was to move Alice's bed and things and their bedding to the house once they had a dry afternoon.

She hadn't forgotten about their apple orchard. The very next night, when he came into the restaurant for dinner through a pouring rain, she held out her hand, palm up.

"Look what Ciara gave me!"

Jesse glanced down at the little pile of apple seeds, then up into her beaming face. "Well done. I have some in a sack. We'll add these to them."

"Could we measure a row?" she begged.

Jesse shook his head. "We could when it stops raining, but the mud will likely just seep back into place. We shouldn't plant until spring. It can get cold enough around here that the seeds would freeze."

Alice had nodded. It was rather gratifying that his wife expected him to know such things. And even more gratifying to spend the evening listening to her sweet voice reading of daring adventures. It wasn't a bad existence.

But the letter from his parents reminded him there could be more.

Ciara handed it to him when he came in from work

on Thursday, chilled and soaked. "James wanted to make sure you received it. He says it's from Olympia."

By the look in her eyes, she must think it was something from the Territorial Government, but he recognized the hand. "My father," he told her before stepping aside and opening it.

Congratulations on marrying! What great news! We're sorry to have missed the wedding, but we would love to welcome her to the family. When can you come see us?

Alice opened the door and entered the inn just then, shaking her umbrella before turning to smile to him and Ciara. She'd have to take time away from the school to make the journey to Puget City and back. That would probably be inconvenient. And Drew needed him if they were to fulfill their orders.

All those were excuses. He knew the real reason he hesitated to take Alice to meet his family.

They would see what he tried to ignore.

He and his wife weren't in love.

Yet.

CHAPTER TWELVE

ALICE HAD BEEN to one or two town meetings in Cawthorn. There hadn't been many more than that in the last few years. The Cawthorn family ran things, and the meetings were mostly an opportunity to tout their good works. Other opinions were not welcome. Anyone who thought differently either grumbled in private or left town.

The meeting at Wallin Landing couldn't have been more different.

For one thing, benches and chairs had been set up in a circle so everyone could see everyone else. She settled on a bench next to Jesse and watched as various Wallin family members and others in the community found seats as well. In Cawthorn, only those who had reached their majority were allowed to attend and often only the men came. Here citizens as young as fifteen and as old as seventy were present, male and female, filling the hall with a jumble of voices. Wallin Landing may have been founded by the Wallin family, and Wallins managed the store, post office, library, and dispensary, but everyone was allowed an opinion, and there were quite a few.

"Making this place a real town means taxes," one farmer, a Mr. Merganser, complained, rising to address the other attendees. He was thin and craggy, as if life had already trimmed any excess. "I don't know about you, but I came West to avoid things like that."

"And I came West to avoid politics," another man proclaimed, hopping to his feet. Dark-skinned and curly-haired, he had identified himself earlier as Dawes Cooper, one of the miners who had a claim along the upper end of the lake.

"Who's going to run for mayor and city council?" Mrs. Potterby asked. "We had enough trouble getting a schoolboard together."

"She has a claim between here and the Outlet," Jesse whispered to Alice. "Lost her husband last winter."

Alice could only admire the scrappy lady for continuing, especially as she lived out nearly as far as the claim where Katie Jo had been raised, on the stream that ran from the lake to Puget Sound.

But her comment prompted Mrs. Volland to stand up.

"My point entirely," she said with a sniff. "We have a perfectly good schoolboard. We can just broaden their responsibilities. We don't need to make this a town."

Calls for and against circled the room.

"Can the schoolboard do that?" Alice whispered to Jesse, and he shook his head, but more in puzzlement than in answer, she thought.

As Mrs. Volland sat with a flourish, Mr. Bradshaw spoke up from his seat a little to their right. "I volunteered to run for the schoolboard to help the school. I don't have time for endless board meetings over property squabbles and sanitation issues."

Voices rose even higher, riding over each other, until they were nothing but a clash of calls. Jesse reached for her hand.

Drew rose. He held up his hands, and quiet slowly fell.

"Sounds like we have a lot of ideas on how this might come about, or not," he said. "We need to know more about what incorporation entails before we can decide whether it's the right course for all of us." He turned to look at someone near him. "Mr. Hitchcock, could you explain the process?"

"Very smart," Alice whispered to Jesse. "He'll know what to do."

For some reason, her husband merely grunted.

Mr. Hitchcock climbed up onto the stage at one end of the hall. Those closest swiveled in their seats as if to keep him in sight. He stood tall and confident with his hair pomaded back from his face. She tried not to notice how much he resembled Roland.

"Ladies," he said with a nod around, "gentlemen. For those of you who don't know me, I'm Dixon Hitchcock, a lawyer with experience in Territorial ordinance. I've recently moved to Wallin Landing, so I have a vested interest in the outcome of this decision."

He paused as if to make sure they understood. Alice smiled her encouragement.

"If we want to incorporate Wallin Landing as a town," he continued, "we would need to petition the Territorial Legislature at next year's session. They would expect to see a map of our geographical limits, a statement on the form of government we will be using, a list of our town departments and the temporary officials who are staffing them until elections can be held, and how we intend to hold those elections, with candidates for each position, within the next four months. The Legislature would then vote on a law to allow our incorporation."

So simple? Why, that could be done in a short time if everyone agreed.

But they didn't appear to agree at the moment. In fact, many were shaking their heads.

"That's a lot of work," Mr. Bradshaw said as if voicing everyone's concern.

"Port Townsend managed it in 1860," Mr. Hitchcock told him. "Walla Walla received its charter in 1862."

So, it could be done. Alice sat taller. Jesse frowned at her as if he wasn't sure why she was so excited.

"But they're a lot bigger than we are," Mr. Cooper put in. "Leastwise, so I've heard."

"We would need a number of citizens to agree," Mr. Hitchcock allowed. "As many as two hundred and fifty of voting age."

"Do we have two hundred and fifty people of voting age?" Mr. Merganser asked, glancing around as if counting heads.

"Two hundred and sixty were enrolled for the schoolboard election," Catherine supplied. "But that included everyone in a half-day's walk of the school, which might encompass a larger area than what we'd want to consider as the town limits."

Voices started building again.

Alice looked to Jesse. "I think we should try."

His frown eased. "So do I."

Alice straightened and raised her hand. Drew must have noticed, for his deep voice cut through the other sounds. "Yes, Mrs. Willets?"

She still hadn't accustomed herself to that name. As the voices quieted again, Alice rose, feeling all gazes turn her way. "It isn't such a great deal of work once we reach agreement on the details. The greatest effort will likely be the need for meticulous documentation. I would be honored to serve as secretary to the committee."

Several people smiled in her direction as she resumed her seat. Jesse took one of her hands and gave it a squeeze of support.

"Thank you," Drew said. "I'm sure that will be a big help. Are there others who'd like to volunteer their services?"

"I'd be happy to serve as advisor," Mr. Hitchcock offered, stepping down from the stage.

Mrs. Volland popped to her feet. "The schoolboard must be represented. I will serve as committee chair."

Alice sucked in a breath.

Jesse stood up, letting go of her hand in the process. Alice blinked in surprise. As if everyone else was just as shocked, they went silent.

"A Wallin dreamed of this settlement," he said. "Wallins built this settlement. A Wallin should chair the committee. I nominate Mr. Drew Wallin."

He sank back onto the bench to thunderous applause. Alice put her hand on his, finding it trembling. " Well done," she murmured.

His smile was tight, but he nodded.

"Wallins don't have to do everything around here!" Mrs. Volland cried, but her husband tugged on her arm, and she returned to her seat as well.

In the end, everyone agreed that Mr. Merganser would represent the farming community on the committee, Mr. Cooper would represent the miners, and Ciara would represent the businesses. Drew could speak for the loggers. Mrs. Volland was allowed to stay on the committee to represent the school.

But what was particularly lovely was the number of people who stopped to thank Alice's husband for speaking his mind. Jesse kept bobbing his head to their praise, but she could see that it pleased him.

The sun was shining as they came out of the hall. From a nearby claim came the unmistakable **toot** of a willow bark whistle, which Alice had begun distributing that week. She squeezed Jesse's hand. "I think we just have time to carry our things to the cabin."

His smile broadened. "Ciara says she has some starter for bread. I'll stop by the inn and pick it up. Meet you at the school."

The plan decided, she swept across the clearing, heart light. Her new home. It wasn't one she had expected, but one where she had every opportunity for respect and camaraderie if not the love she had once dreamed about. Then again, something was growing between her and Jesse. It was quite possible all her dreams were about to come true.

A man was standing on the steps of the school, hand raised as if he had knocked on the door. That elegant frame, the well-tailored clothing, the golden hair peeking out from under his tall hat. Dixon Hitchcock was still in the hall. This couldn't be …

He turned and met her gaze, and her stomach dropped into her half boots.

"Roland?"

Jesse ambled into the inn, feeling nothing but pleased. Not a single person had questioned Alice's offer to serve as secretary to the new incorporation committee. They could see her intelligence, her candor, her ability to put words together. She ought to be the one writing books!

And he was still a little surprised nearly everyone had approved of his idea to have Drew lead the committee. Most folks liked Drew, but not everyone liked or even knew Jesse. It was nice to have his idea appreciated too.

He came through the kitchen door to find Ciara bending over the pot she must have left simmering. "I'll get that starter for you in just a moment, Jesse," she called, stirring.

"Take your time." He leaned on the sideboard by the sink. "That sure smells good."

"Corn chowder," she said, peering down into the kettle as if judging the food within. "We had plenty of cream, so it made sense." She grinned at him. "You can tell me if it tastes as good as it smells after dinner."

Jesse grinned back. "Deal."

He turned and glanced out the window toward the

school, then frowned. Across the clearing, Alice stood toe to toe with some fellow. His face was growing redder, and hers was growing whiter.

"Who's that?" he asked, tipping his chin.

"Mr. Cawthorn from back East," Ciara said. "I understand he's only staying the night. Jesse?"

He heard the last as the kitchen door slammed behind him. Cawthorn? As in Roland Cawthorn? As in the idiot who had thrown his Alice away for another woman who could in no way be her equal? His legs ate up the ground between the inn and the school.

Whoever he was, Jesse didn't like the look on Alice's face. It reminded him of how she'd looked when Mrs. Volland had scolded her about the storm, when he'd volunteered to marry her. No one got to make his wife look like that.

He towered over Alice, glaring at the fellow.

The man reared back. "What is this?"

Alice turned and saw Jesse, and he could almost feel the fear melting away. She latched onto his arm as if she'd never let go.

"Jesse." His name was a blessing and a cry for help.

He set his hand over hers. "Alice."

She spared the newcomer a look. "Mr. Cawthorn, I fear you've come all this way for nothing. Allow me to introduce you to Jesse Willets. My husband."

Jesse stood beside her, strong, proud, and Alice knew she was safe. Yet Roland's ultimatum still rang in her ears.

"My dear Alice," he'd greeted when she had first discovered him in front of the school. "I'm so glad I found you at last." He'd made it sound as if he'd traveled as far as the North Pole searching for her.

"What are you doing here?" she'd asked.

"Why, I've come to bring you home." He'd stepped

down to run his hands up her arms. "Darling, I made a terrible mistake. I don't know what came over me. But I've realized that you're the only one for me. Please, say you'll forgive me and return home."

"No." Alice had pulled away from him. "No, Roland. This is home now."

"This?" He'd waved a hand and laughed, laughed! at Wallin Landing. "You cannot be serious. You were raised for so much more."

"Yes," she'd agreed. "Respect, devotion, constancy."

He had had the good sense to grimace. "I can see you're still upset with me. You have every right. But if you allow me to escort you home, I will prove to you that I am a changed man."

"No," she repeated. "I am not leaving. Good day, sir."

He'd caught her arm as she'd attempted to push past him for the school, and his eyes had narrowed to slits of ice. "How dare you speak to me that way! Your parents and brother would be ashamed. Do you know the trouble I've been through because of you? You *will* come with me. Now."

And then Jesse, dear Jesse, had formed a wall beside her. She clung to his arm now.

Roland stared at her. "Your husband."

"Married by clergy a little over a week ago," Jesse rumbled.

Roland sucked in an audible breath. Then he stormed across the clearing, and she heard the door of the inn slam behind him.

"Well," she said.

"Would you like me to punch him?" Jesse asked.

Laughter bubbled up despite the situation. "No, thank you, Jesse. But I'm very glad you came along when you did."

"Saw you across the clearing," he said. "Didn't like the look of things."

"I'm sure I looked as if I'd seen a ghost." She shivered, and he put an arm about her shoulders. She leaned into the strength, the warmth, inhaling the scent of clean cotton and wool.

"Do you still love him?"

The question jerked her out of his arms. "What? No! He's a faithless brute."

Jesse nodded. "Good."

"Yes," Alice said. "That's very good." She glanced at the inn. "I hope your declaration was sufficient to deter him from further contact. I'd truly prefer not to have to deal with him again."

"You won't have to," Jesse said. "Tell Rina you need a few days off."

Alice looked back at her husband. His face was pale, but his chin was up, and he clearly had settled on a solution.

"Why?" she asked. "It won't take that much time to move our last few things into the cabin."

"We can finish that today," he confirmed. "And tomorrow, after services, we'll head for Seattle and book passage on a steamer heading south. My parents want to meet you. Now's a good time."

He was probably right. If she disappeared for a few days, Roland would probably give up and return home.

But somehow, she thought she'd just been lifted from the frying pan into the fire.

Jesse stayed close to Alice the rest of the afternoon and evening. He stood at the door of James and Rina's cabin while she requested some time away from the school. When the Wallins heard she wanted to meet Jesse's family, they were quick to agree. Then, as the light began to fade, he and Alice carried their things to the cabin.

Drew had been surprised when Jesse had mentioned building the second bedstead.

"You won't be needing it for at least nine months," he'd teased.

"Company might come calling," Jesse had told him.

So now, the cabin had a bed in each of its sleeping rooms. He was looking forward to being able to lie down without curling up his legs, but he knew he'd miss the sound of Alice breathing.

He cooked dinner over the hearth. The beans and ham weren't as good as Ciara's, but Alice ate them and praised his work, which made them sweeter still. As she was settling by the fire, he rose.

"Going to the inn a moment. Be right back." He left before she could question him.

Dixon Hitchcock often ate at the inn, so Jesse wasn't surprised to find him at the smallest table near the stairs to the upper story. Roland Cawthorn must have eaten already, for Jesse caught no sign of him. He doubted the Easterner would venture out of the inn after dark, even if he knew the way to Jesse and Alice's claim, but he wasn't about to take that chance. Best he get his talking done and quick.

"Mind if I sit?" he asked the lawyer.

Hitchcock waved at the opposite chair. "Be my guest."

Jesse folded himself onto the seat. "I need the services of a lawman or a lawyer. We don't have our own constable, so I thought of you."

"Happy to help," he said, laying down his spoon as if to give Jesse his full attention.

"There's a man staying at the inn, Roland Cawthorn," Jesse explained. "He followed Alice here from Boston. They come from Cawthorn, a town named after his family. He hurt her, real bad. That's why she left home to come here."

The lawyer's look darkened. "I dislike him already. Go on."

"I want to know why he came," Jesse said. "Alice says he wanted her forgiveness. It seemed to me more like he was threatening her, trying to force her to return. He's rich and powerful, by all accounts. Why chase her all the way to the other side of the country when he'd thrown her over with less care than a broken saw?"

Hitchcock nodded. "I have friends back East, some in the Boston area. I'll see what I can learn."

Jesse reached into his pocket and drew out some money. "I can pay you."

The lawyer held up his hand. "No need. Consider it my wedding gift to you if it saves that dear lady a moment of concern."

"Much obliged," Jesse said, pulling back. "We're heading down the Sound tomorrow. Might not be back for a few days, maybe a week."

"By then, I hope to be able to lay the issue of Mr. Cawthorn's sudden appearance to rest," he promised.

CHAPTER THIRTEEN

SITTING IN THEIR little cabin in the woods, it was easy for Alice to pretend Roland Cawthorn and her parents didn't exist. She had pulled the two chairs up near the fire, which was crackling nicely, thanks to Jesse. Thanks to Harry and Kit too. They'd helped him stock the woodpile next to the house. Ciara had once told her that that was how a logger expressed his love, by chopping wood.

She frowned. There was a towering pile of wood outside. Did that mean Jesse loved her?

Suddenly, it wasn't only the fire keeping her warm. He was so shy and quiet. Would he tell her his feelings? Could she trust them? What if she came to rely on them and they dwindled to nothing, just like Roland's supposed affections for her?

Reality galloped back. Roland had crossed the continent to bring her home. Why? She couldn't believe he was truly sorry or that he had suddenly come to his senses. It had taken her two months after he'd thrown her over to make all the arrangements to leave Cawthorn. Two months of being pitied and scorned. Two months of watching him make cow eyes at his new sweetheart as he introduced her to everyone in town. Two months of being berated and told to try to make it up to him, as if she were the one at fault.

Two months was plenty of time to change a mind. It had been enough to change her life.

She heard boots on the porch a moment before the door opened and Jesse entered.

Alice put off her brooding and smiled at him. "How are things at the inn?"

He came to hold his hands out to the fire. "Fine."

"Nothing needing your attention?" she probed.

"No."

She puffed out a sigh. "You left in a hurry, Jesse. It's only natural I would wonder why."

He lowered himself onto the chair next to hers. His cheeks were reddening, but it might have been the reflected glow of the fire.

"Just making arrangements," he said. "Ciara tells me Hart and Beth McCormick are coming out for services tomorrow. Likely we can ride with them to the city to catch the steamer south."

Beth McCormick was the Wallin sister. Alice had only met her twice since moving to Wallin Landing. Between her fashionable gowns and her sunny demeanor, it was impossible not to like her. "That would be lovely. I look forward to becoming better acquainted."

He nodded, gaze on the fire. Had the meeting with Roland unsettled him too? Perhaps she should raise a different topic.

"I'm also looking forward to meeting your family," she said. "You mentioned that your father raises cattle, and you have nine siblings. Do they all live at the ranch?"

"For now," he said. "My next two oldest brothers want their own places, but they've been staying close to help Pa."

Helping apparently ran in the family. She could think of worse traits to inherit. "And your sisters?"

He shifted on the seat as if trying to get comfortable.

She would have to see about sewing some pillows to cushion the hard wood. She could do that, at least!

"Maybe I should explain a little," he said at last. "I'm the oldest. Jack's a year younger, with Jeremy a year behind him, and Jacob two years behind."

Alice stifled a giggle. "Jesse, Jack, Jeremy, and Jacob? Your parents must like names that start with J."

He grinned. "Pa's named Joseph, and Ma's named Julia, you see. They thought it would be fun to have all of us with the same letter."

Alice raised her brows. "All ten?"

"Yes, ma'am. After Jacob comes Jane. She's one and twenty now. Two years after her is Jenny, then Joanna at seventeen. Jason will be fifteen before Christmas, and Joshua will be fourteen next fall. My littlest sister is Joy. She's ten."

Which meant he was nearly old enough to be Joy's father. "I can only admire your mother," she said. "I have eight children in my classroom, and I know how difficult it can be to keep up with them all."

"She told me once she was thankful they came in batches. I was ten when Jane was born, and she was ten when Joy was born. Ma said that was the good Lord giving her room to learn and grow."

Alice beamed. "What a lovely way to look at it."

"Always thought I'd like a big family," he mused, then he hastily straightened. "But just being a couple is fine too. Fewer little ones underfoot."

The truth bit hard. If she insisted on a marriage of convenience, there would be no little ones underfoot. Orphans were fairly rare here, from what she understood, and families generally adopted them quickly. Did she truly want to spend her life teaching other people's children and never her own?

Between Roland's unexpected appearance and their discussion before bed, the thoughts swirling in her head made sleep difficult that night. Still, she managed to rise in time to perform her morning ablutions and dress for church. Jesse seemed to have guessed she would want to avoid the inn again this morning, for he had cut some slices from a loaf of good brown bread Ciara had given them and was toasting them on a long-handled fork over the fire when she came out of her room.

"Coffee's about ready," he told her, and she inhaled the nutty aroma.

"You will have to teach me," she said, taking the chair next to his.

"You'll catch on fast," he assured her. He handed her the fork. "You already know something about toasting bread. Keep the fork turning slowly back and forth. That way the toast browns without burning."

She should have asked him before she'd tried toasting breakfast for him the other day! This time, she managed to produce several golden-brown slices, which they slathered with butter and black raspberry preserves, again courtesy of Ciara.

A short time later, they made their way back into the main clearing and up the hill to the church. Rain had washed everything in the night, leaving behind a cool, crisp scent that told her winter was not far off.

Thank goodness she'd decided to wear a warmer coat on her trip West. The heavy navy wool fell to the top edge of her bottom flounce, and the wide collar, cuffs, overskirt, and hem were covered in a thick band of mink. Her mother had insisted on the expense. Dressing well was a mark that Alice was in Roland's class. She would never have considered Alice might need it for more practical purposes.

Of course Roland had decided to attend services as well. He was out in front of the little chapel, surrounded by a group of people who seemed to be hanging on his every word. Worse, Mrs. Volland was hanging on his arm, seemingly oblivious to her husband's glower. Alice studiously ignored them as Jesse led her into the church and they found seats about in the middle. And she managed to focus on the service and sermon, with no more than an occasional look to where Roland sat, proud and pious, on the opposite side of the aisle.

But Mrs. Volland was not about to let well enough alone. As everyone came out of services, she hurried over to Alice and Jesse.

"Mr. Cawthorn is such a gentleman," she warbled, gaze going to where Roland was attempting to engage Drew and Catherine in conversation. Of course he would have identified the most respected family and seek to cozy up. "Why didn't you tell me you had such impressive friends from the East, Mrs. Willets?"

"Because I don't," Alice said politely. "Mr. Cawthorn and I are not friends."

Jesse looked away, as if to hide a smile.

Mrs. Volland's face, however, puckered. "But he came all this way to fetch you home."

How did she know? Alice exchanged glances with Jesse, then focused on the schoolboard chair again. "Did he tell you that?"

"Not in so many words," she admitted. "But he wrote to the schoolboard some time ago asking us to release you from your duties. He offered to pay us a very tidy sum if we let you go. I didn't share it with the rest of the board. I didn't want to embarrass you."

Alice stared at her. "Then that's why you kept trying to get me to resign!"

Others were turning their way. Jesse shifted as if to protect her from their view.

"I was trying to do you a favor," Mrs. Volland huffed. "Just think, young lady. You could have married that!" She looked to where Roland was laughing over something someone must have said.

Alice latched onto Jesse's arm. "Instead, I married a man who is constant and true. I think I made a very fine choice. Excuse us." She tugged her husband down the hill and away from the lady's insults.

As they rode out of Wallin Landing in the McCormick buckboard Sunday afternoon to a chorus of willow bark whistles, Jesse kept looking back. Beth and Hart had indeed been delighted to take them in to Seattle and let them spend the night, as the steamer south wouldn't leave until the Monday morning tide. He just kept expecting to see Roland Cawthorn riding after them.

"I'm so glad you two decided to marry," Beth told them as Hart guided the wagon down the track through the woods. The shadows of the firs made the road seem cooler, quieter. "Didn't I tell you that you should have been the one to fetch Alice from the harbor, Jesse?"

Alice, who was seated beside him in the bed of the wagon, looked at him askance.

"You told me," Jesse said to Beth, who was riding on the bench with her husband, dressed in a pink and white gown nearly as fancy as Alice's beaded blue gown. "At the time, Harry wanted it more. We arm-wrestled for it, and he won."

Alice stared at him. "You fought for the right to bring me to the settlement?"

It might be November, but he felt as if the heat of summer was bearing down on him. "Not much of a fight, and I lost."

"You ended up bringing her anyway," Beth reminded him with a laugh and a toss of her golden curls. "And Harry married Katie Jo."

"Mrs. McCormick is something of a matchmaker," Jesse explained to Alice. "She likes to see folks getting hitched."

"I like to see true love triumph," Beth corrected him. "There's nothing so satisfying as having a hand in that." She sighed happily, then tucked her hand into her husband's arm.

For a taciturn lawman with dark hair and steely gray eyes, Hart McCormick sure could smile at his wife.

Now Alice was pinking as well. "And who will come to retrieve us when we return?" she asked Jesse.

"Whoever comes in for the mail that day," he allowed. "I told Kit we probably wouldn't be back before Thursday, so, starting that day, they'll be driving in the wagon, just in case."

Alice beamed at him. "Very wise."

Beth swiveled to look back at them again. "Do you follow *Godey's*, Alice?"

They were already calling each other by their first names, as if they'd known each other for years. Beth was like that. Sometimes, he wished *he* was like that. Best he could do was to let the ladies talk as the wagon bumped along the road, which had been cleared of storm debris.

Hart also remained quiet. The deputy sheriff, he tended to keep his own **counsel**. Jesse understood.

The only issue came when they reached the McCormick home in Seattle. It was a fine two-story clapboard house with a covered front porch that looked out over the city. Hart drove the buckboard around to the stable at the back. While he saw to the horses, Jesse helped Alice and Beth down. Arm in arm, heads close together, the two ladies headed for the kitchen door.

Hart tipped up his chin as he started unhitching the horses. "I figured those two would get along."

"Me too," Jesse said as the door shut behind them. He went to help Hart release the chains. "You have one extra bedroom, don't you?"

The lawman nodded as he worked. "That a problem?"

"You mind if I sleep on the porch?" Jesse asked.

Hart glanced toward the house. "You in trouble with your bride already?"

"No," Jesse allowed. "It's just the way we arranged things."

Hart frowned, but he didn't question him further. "Sleep wherever you like. There's extra blankets in the chest at the foot of the bed."

That settled, and after the horses were let out to pasture, Jesse loped down to the telegraph office to send a wire to his family. Someone would need to be waiting at the dock in Puget City when they got off. The town might have a fancy name, but it consisted only of two stores, a sawmill, a restaurant, and a saloon. He couldn't count on anyone having horses to borrow, much less a sidesaddle for Alice.

Beth made them a savory dinner of ham slices, mashed potatoes and gravy, and her family's signature biscuits. Alice had stationed herself in the kitchen during the preparations as if to watch every move.

"She's learning to cook," Jesse explained when Hart frowned in that direction.

He was only glad that Alice didn't seem to notice the issue of the bedroom until it was time to retire. When they reached the door of the room, she turned and stared at Jesse. "What do we do?"

"Already settled," he promised her. "I just need to grab a few things from our valise."

He did so and left her. She had an odd look on her face, and he wasn't sure whether she was relieved or confused by his arrangements.

But she was at his side when he purchased two tickets on the *Northern Star* for Puget City the next morning. Mist shrouded Elliott Bay as a sailor rowed them and two other men out to the ship, the sound of the oars hushed. Other sailors took Alice's arms and lifted her to the deck, while Jesse handed up their valise. Then he and the other passengers climbed up the short rope ladder to join her.

Jesse gripped the valise in one hand and put his other hand to Alice's back to escort her down the rail. Even swathed in that fur-studded coat, better than most ladies saw their whole lives, she seemed fragile.

"You cold?" he asked. "We could go inside the cabin."

She turned toward the long white block in the center of the two-deck ship with the pilot house at the top of one end. Already smoke puffed out of two of the open windows. Some gents must be enjoying cigars.

"I'm fine," she said, turning back to the city.

With a grunt of machinery and the shush of water, the big sidewheel began turning, and the ship backed out toward Puget Sound. A moment later and the pipes began their tune.

Alice's brows went up. "Is that an organ?"

Jesse chuckled. "Calliope. See the brass pipes lined up by the pilot house? Steam fuels them just like the paddlewheel."

Alice studied the pilot house. "I see them! And Yankee Doodle. How marvelous!"

"I hear the Brits at Victoria don't think so," Jesse told her. "But the machinery was never set up to play God Save the Queen."

Alice's laughter and the metallic call of the calliope played them out of the harbor.

Dark smoke belched from the tall black stack of the white-sided steamer as they chugged south. Clouds draped the hills and forests, hiding the Olympics to the west and the Cascades to the east. A salmon jumped, flashing silver from the cold gray waters, and an eagle swooped low to snatch it up.

Alice stuck her hands into the sleeves of her coat and hugged the material closer.

"You sure you don't want to go inside?" Jesse asked. "I could ask them not to smoke."

She shook her head. "I don't mind the cold. I'm just amazed by the grandeur. Everything about Puget Sound is different from where I grew up."

"It's mighty pretty," he allowed. "Just like you."

He wasn't sure where that had come from, for all it was the truth, but she turned to him, dimples making an appearance. "Why, thank you, Jesse. I can think of little praise more honoring than to be compared to Nature's beauty."

And wasn't he just the cleverest fellow to think of it?

He didn't feel nearly as clever when they got off the steamer onto the wide plank dock at Puget City. The whir of the nearby sawmill drowned out the thud of their steps as they walked to the shore, where the road ran along clapboard buildings at the foot of the plateau. From the saloon came the plunk of a piano. Alice picked her skirts up out of the mud.

"Here he comes! Here he comes!"

He would never mistake his littlest sister's voice, sweet and piping. Turning toward the sound, he spotted Jacob, his third brother, standing by the wagon in front of Bill Egbert's store. Anyone looking would have guessed they were related, for they all had some version of his father's russet hair. His brother Jason was holding the horses, and Joy was perched on the bench.

"There's my family," he told Alice with a nod in their direction.

Joy pointed. "Look how pretty she is!"

Alice linked her arm with his. "I see quiet doesn't necessarily run in the family."

She didn't know the half of it. And it dawned on him that he might have been better off staying in Wallin Landing.

CHAPTER FOURTEEN

"YOU MUST BE a nice schoolmarm," Jesse's sister Joy said, gazing up at Alice from the bed of the wagon. "Cuz you're so pretty."

The little girl had copper-colored ringlets framing a round face and eyes as deep a gray as the waters on which Alice had just sailed. She smiled shyly at Alice, fingers pleating her pink gingham skirts, but Jesse's brother Jacob, who was seated next to Alice at the reins, snorted.

Jesse, on her other side, leaned around her with a frown. "You don't think my wife is pretty?"

His brother sat straighter. He was leaner than Jesse, and his gaze was partially hidden by a pair of wire-rimmed spectacles. He too had russet hair like her husband sticking out from under his flat-brimmed straw hat. His shirt was blue gingham instead of flannel, but his trousers and sturdy boots looked just like Jesse's too.

"She's plenty pretty," he told Jesse. "But pretty on the outside doesn't mean pretty on the inside." He made a face and glanced to Alice. "No offense, ma'am."

"None taken," Alice assured him. "I completely agree with your assessment, Mr. Willets. We should judge people by their actions, not their outer appearance."

"But you *are* a nice schoolmarm, aren't you?" Joy asked, voice now beginning to sound less sure.

"There are no nice schoolmarms," his brother Jason

warned, sprawled out in the bed beside Joy. His hair was a darker shade, as if determined to match his cynical outlook, and his build was stockier.

Joy's face melted.

Jesse swiveled to meet his sister's gaze. "Jason's wrong. Alice is the nicest schoolmarm you'd ever want to meet. All her students love her."

Joy sighed happily, and Alice was hard-pressed not to do the same.

Jacob guided the horses out of the little town to climb through stumps and fern into a forest that smelled of rain and fir.

"How far is it to your ranch?" Alice asked her new brother-in-law.

Jacob was focused on the horses, a pair of roans that might well have been chosen to match the family's coloring. "About a half mile. You'll know we're getting close when the forest opens into prairie."

"Call me if you spot anything worthwhile," Jason said, slumping into the bed and pulling his hat down over his eyes.

"What do you consider worthwhile?" Alice asked.

His hat bobbed as he answered. "Deer, elk, moose."

"Jason's a good hunter," Jesse explained.

"Though I doubt we'll see a moose," Jacob added. "They prefer to forage down on the delta."

"Worse luck," Jason muttered.

"When we get to the prairie, I'm going to pick you wildflowers, Alice," Joy announced.

"The wildflowers faded months ago, Joy," Jacob said, pausing to cluck to the horses to pick up their paces.

"There might be some pearly everlasting," Joy protested.

"We had holly at our wedding," Alice told her. "Jesse thought of it because all the flowers were gone at Wallin Landing too." She shared a smile with her husband.

"Ma said it was an odd time of year to marry," Jacob said. "And in a hurry too."

The bench felt much harder all of a sudden.

"How is Ma?" Jesse asked, and she could only be glad of the change in topic.

He asked after every one of his family members and neighbors, including the neighbor's dog, as they wound through woods that crowded close on every side. Indeed, in places, the stumps of their fallen brothers still stood sentinel in the middle of the road, testimony as to how recently it had been blazed. Alice tried to listen to Jacob's answers, hoping to gather some idea of who she was soon to meet, but the sway of the wagon and the drone of voices made it hard to keep her eyes open.

Then the forest brightened, the trees dwindled, and all at once, they were out on a wide prairie, where golden-brown grasses swayed and rattled in the breeze. Here and there, she spotted **farmhouses** in the distance.

"Almost home!" Joy sang out, and Jason stirred.

Jacob turned onto a rutted drive that cut through the prairie. On either side, reddish lumps raised their heads to gaze at them with wide eyes.

"Even your cattle are red!" Alice realized. Then she blushed.

They all laughed.

"Ruby reds," Jason said. "They were good enough for George Washington, so they're good enough for us."

"Our first president favored the breed," Jacob explained. "Pa bought some off another settler when we first arrived in the area."

"He tried for some of the black Spanish cattle at Fort Nisqually," Jason added, "but they wouldn't sell to an American. Brits." He shook his head.

"Is the fort close?" Alice asked, glancing around. Some sort of tower stood to the east of them, a solid block rising off the prairie.

"On the other side of the delta," Jesse supplied. "But it's a far piece to walk and hard to cross the rivers at certain times of the year."

"That's the blockhouse," Jacob said as if he'd noticed her look.

"Built during the Indian War," Jason added. "For protection."

"But we don't need it now," Jesse said quellingly, and his brother fell silent.

Ahead, she could see a two-story farmhouse, twin barns, and several outbuildings. Built of clapboard and painted white, they looked neat and tidy among the waving grasses.

The Willets family were not quite so neat and tidy. In fact, the words Alice would have chosen were busy and boisterous.

They all spilled out of the various buildings to meet them. She could see where Jesse got his russet hair. His father's was a brighter shade than his, with gray at the temples. His mother's was a warm brown, gray threading through the bun on top of her head. All the oldest three brothers could look Jesse in the eye, and one of his sisters reached the tip of his nose. The brothers wore gingham shirts, the sisters gingham dresses, some belted at the waist with leather, others covered in aprons.

Jesse jumped down, but one of the other brothers, Jeremy, she was guessing, reached up to help her before Jesse had a moment to turn. Another had already taken possession of their valise.

"Welcome to the family, Alice!" Jesse's mother cried, opening her arms.

Alice stepped into the hug, and she was certain she heard her stays creak at the warm pressure. Certainly it was hard to catch her breath as she leaned back. But more hugs followed, from his sisters, from his father.

"I'm Jack," said the one with the valise, extending his hand to shake hers.

"And I'm Jeremy," said the one who had helped her down, confirming her suspicions. He favored her with a bow, green eyes twinkling. "And that youngster is Joshua."

Jesse's youngest brother nodded respectfully, thumbs tucked into his suspenders.

"And those are Jane, Jenny, and Joanna," their mother said so rapidly Alice wasn't sure which young lady belonged to which name. "Come on in, now. You must be tired from your travels. I never did know why Jesse felt the need to move so far away from us." She gave her oldest a look as she turned for the door of the house.

"Especially since we're all so accommodating," Jeremy said, holding the door for his mother and Alice. He let go in time for it to swing back on Jesse, who caught it with a grunt.

"Never you mind them, Alice," his tallest sister—Jane?—said with a look to her brothers. "They've been teasing each other pretty near since the day they were born."

"At least since the day *I* was born," the sister with the sleekest hair agreed, taking Joy's hand to pull her into the house. "I'm Jenny, by the way, in case Ma confused you."

"And what's your name if Ma didn't confuse her?" Jeremy asked with a grin.

"Jenny," Joy said, frowning. "You know that."

They came into a wide entry, with stairs along one wall leading up. Through the door on the right, Alice could see a huge dining table and enough chairs for fourteen. The door on the left opened into a parlor with a horsehair sofa, a collection of ladder-back chairs with colorful cushions, and bookshelves crammed with tomes. It was clear where Jesse got his love for books.

"Guess what?" Joy asked her milling family. "Alice is a real nice schoolmarm. Jesse said so."

The women and girls all glanced at each other and sighed.

"Surely you have a nice schoolmarm here," Alice protested.

"Yes," Jason put in. "And her name is Ma."

Joshua elbowed him. "And Pa."

Jesse's father laughed. "What they mean, Alice, is that the closest school is too far away for them to walk, so their mother and I taught them."

"Reading, writing, and 'rithmatic," Jenny said.

"Plus everything to manage a farm," Jane added.

"Speaking of which," Jack said, "we should show sister Alice around before it gets too dark." He set down the valise and offered her his arm.

His mother forestalled him. "That can wait for the morning. Jack, take their valise up to their room. Jane, get the cake out of the oven. Jenny, Jason, see that the table is ready. Joanna and the rest of you, come help me in the kitchen."

And just like that, they all vanished, leaving Alice and Jesse alone with his father.

He clapped Jesse on the shoulder. "It's good to have you home, son. You and Alice can wash up in our bedroom before dinner if you'd like."

"Thanks," Jesse said, taking Alice's arm. "This way."

He followed the hall to the last room on the left.

"They're a lot," he acknowledged as they entered a bedroom covered in creamy wallpaper dotted with tiny pink rosebuds. The poster bed had a quilt much like the ones Ma Wallin had made, and there was a washstand with a rose-patterned pitcher and basin in one corner.

"They're dears," Alice said, going to pour water into the basin. "It was only me and Gerald growing up, and he's several years my elder. I would have loved to have a sister to confide in. Why did you want to leave?"

He rubbed his chin, where tiny specks of red stubble

were just beginning to show. "Raising cows didn't feel right. And Pa had plenty of help. I guess I wanted something of my own."

"Like our orchard," she said, shaking the water from her hands.

His smile warmed her. "Like our orchard."

They finished cleaning up and returned to the dining room to find his mother and father standing at the head of the table, their sons and daughters busily laying out plates and cutlery. Mrs. Willets leaned her head on her husband's shoulder, and he pressed a kiss to her hair.

The picture seemed so foreign. She couldn't remember ever seeing her parents kiss. The intimacy seemed just that—intimate, shared privately between married couples.

And yet, why should it be hidden away? Such tenderness was beautiful, something to be admired.

What would it be like if Jesse held her that way, pressed a kiss against her temple, murmured words of love?

He had been so afraid that Alice would be overwhelmed by his family, but he should have realized that she could handle more than one person at a time. She was a schoolmarm! Still, they didn't make it easy on either of them as his father said the blessing and dishes began to pass from hand to hand.

"When did your family come West, Alice?" his mother asked as she plopped a cornbread muffin on his wife's plate.

"Only recently," Alice replied, accepting the bowl of stewed apples from Jane. "I came alone, having responded to an advertisement at Boston Normal, my teachers' college, for a schoolteacher at Wallin Landing."

Jacob perked up. "You attended college. How I envy you."

Jenny, however, stared at her from across the table,

ignoring the platter of chicken Jason was trying to hand her. "You came all this way by yourself? I find that so commendable!"

"Boston," Jane put in worshipfully. "Culture and music and literature. No wonder your clothes are so lovely."

"Thank you," Alice said. "I'm actually from a small town just west of Boston called Cawthorn, though I did live in Boston for a time while I attended college."

"And what does your father do?" his father asked.

"He's head of accounting for Cawthorn Industries, owned by the family who founded the town," she said. "My grandfather held the same position until his death."

"So she comes from a smart family," Jacob put in with a quick glance at Jesse.

Jack had been quiet. Too quiet for Jesse's peace of mind. His next oldest brother usually had to take charge of any situation. He leaned forward now, and Jesse tensed.

"Why did you marry Jesse, Alice?" he asked.

Every bowl and fork stilled. She must have noticed all the looks directed her way, some curious, some eager, because she raised her chin as if to meet them. "Your brother saved me from a terrible storm. He is a hero."

Jesse dropped back in his seat. Was that how she saw him? What had happened to the dull fellow who needed her to explain words? Or could heroes be dull?

"That's our Jesse," Joanna said, slicing into her chicken. "Always there when you need him."

Now his cheeks were surely pink.

"Honest to a fault," Jeremy agreed. "Especially when pointing out your faults."

"Kind and thoughtful, like all my children," his mother insisted. "You should have seen him growing up, Alice. He held Jack's hand to help him walk when he was barely toddling himself."

Jack busied himself with buttering his cornbread.

Jason rolled his eyes. "We've all heard the stories. He

pulled Jeremy away from the fire before he could be burned, and he fought off a bear single-handedly when Jacob decided he was old enough to go pick berries on his own."

Alice gaped at him, brows up and eyes wide.

"It was only a little bear," Jesse said, squeezing his fingers together. "And I was big for my age."

"How old were you?" she asked.

"He was ten," his mother answered for him. "And he scared me half to death, coming home with scratches all over him and his ear nearly chewed off. Haven't you shown her your scar, Jesse?"

Jesse touched the spot behind one ear. "Must have slipped my mind."

"You fought off a bear at ten?" Alice asked, voice awed.

"It was a little bear," Jesse insisted.

"The wild critters learned to leave him alone," his father put in. "And that meant they tended to leave his brothers and sisters alone too. I've always been thankful for Jesse."

Once more, he really wished the floor would open up.

After dinner, half of the family set the kitchen to rights while the other half made sure of the outbuildings and critters. It was his mother's, Jane's, Joshua's, Jason's, and Joy's turn in the kitchen, so they carried off Alice. Jesse joined his father, older brothers, Jenny, and Joanna on the rounds.

"She seems like a fine woman, son," his father said as Jacob and his two older sisters went to milk the few cows kept for that purpose. "I can see why you cottoned to her."

"I still don't understand why she cottoned to *you*," Jeremy said, looping a gate closed as they passed.

"That's enough of that, now," their father said. "Any lady would be proud to wed one of my sons."

"If we could find any ladies," Jeremy reminded him.

Even in vaunted Olympia, just over the horizon, unwed women suitable for marriage were few and far between.

"Speak for yourself," Jack put in. "I'll find a bride in my own time." He nodded to Jesse. "Welcome home, brother. We can talk more in the morning. I have first watch tonight." He started up the stairs to the loft.

Jesse frowned. "Is Jack sleeping out here now?"

His father sighed. "He wanted space of his own. We fixed up a sitting room and bedroom over the barn. It's not much, but it's something."

"If you can stand the smell," Jeremy agreed with a grin.

He and Jacob fell in beside Jesse as they finally headed back toward the house. The sun was an orange glow beyond the Olympics, painting the house and barns in rose.

"Do you like being married?" Jacob asked, adjusting his hold on the pail of milk.

His third closest brother had always been one who wanted to know things. Jesse hadn't minded teaching him growing up, but this was one area where he couldn't find his footing. "I'm still adjusting to it."

"I'd like to adjust to it," Jeremy said. "Particularly with a lady as pretty and sweet as your Alice. But the last unmarried lady in these parts was an eighty-year-old widow who favored chawing tobacco." He shuddered.

"There's always mail-order brides," Jesse suggested. "Some of the men around Seattle have had good luck with them."

Jacob frowned, but Jeremy nodded thoughtfully. "I've been wondering about that."

"Ma would never stand for it," Jacob warned him. "You know how she feels about marrying for love."

The truth dug a hole in Jesse's heart.

By the time they returned to the house and poured the milk into canisters in the cellar to keep cool, everyone was heading for bed. Jesse climbed the stairs with Alice, following his younger sisters.

"We're giving you our room," Joy told them. "It has the most space and the biggest bed."

Alice's smile was frozen to her face. "Why, how considerate, but I wouldn't want to put you out."

"You're not," Joanna insisted, passing them as they came out on the landing. "We're bunking in with Jane and Jenny tonight. I predict no sleep will be had by any of us because we can talk *all* night." She wiggled her brows before continuing down the hall.

Jesse opened the door and let Alice into the room. "Sorry," he said, eying the big, timber-framed bed with its colorful quilt. "I didn't think to tell them." He wouldn't have known how to tell them. "I'll sleep on the floor."

Alice squared her shoulders. "No. There's room. Just stay on your side."

He swallowed. "Yes, ma'am."

He stepped outside so she could change.

Jason was coming up the stairs. He frowned at Jesse. "Something wrong?"

"No."

He shrugged and continued on to the room he shared with Joshua.

A few moments later, Jane came up. She too frowned. "Everything all right?"

"Yes."

He was just glad Alice called the all clear before any of the rest of his family noticed. He'd have to tell them about his loveless marriage at some point.

But not tonight.

CHAPTER FIFTEEN

ALICE DIDN'T REMEMBER falling asleep. She had lain on her back, arms at her sides, careful not to bump into Jesse in any way as he lay beside her. She heard his breathing, steady and strong; felt the straw mattress give as he must have shifted. She said her evening prayers and added one more.

Help me know Thy will, Father, when it comes to this man who's been placed in my life.

And then she woke up, cuddled by strength.

She sank into the feeling. She was pressed against Jesse's side, and one of his arms was around her, holding her close. Her brain informed her she ought to be embarrassed, but she silenced it. How could she feel embarrassed by something so **sheltering**, so tender? She sighed and burrowed closer, and his arm tightened, as if he'd never let her go.

She didn't want him to let her go.

Outside, in the hallway, voices murmured and footsteps thumped against wood. His chest still rose and fell rhythmically. Should she wake him? Should she move?

Slowly, she levered herself up. Cinnamon-colored lashes swept his cheeks, and his mouth was soft with sleep. Before she knew what she was about, she bent and pressed her lips to his. They felt as soft as they looked, warming under hers.

And then they firmed, and both arms came around her, and she was spiraling into joy.

A moment, an eternity later, she pulled back and met his gaze, as round as her own likely was.

For a moment, they just stared at each other.

"Do you want to…" he started.

"Breakfast," she said, joy popping like a bubble and panic surging up behind it. "I smell bacon. We shouldn't keep your family waiting." She wiggled to her side of the bed and tugged the covers up over her head. After a moment of silence, he rose. His clothing rustled as he must have thrown it on, then the door shut behind him.

She climbed out of bed and dressed with trembling fingers. Why was she so shaken? He hadn't stolen that kiss. She'd been the one to kiss him. There was no reason to feel guilty. There was nothing wrong with kissing your own husband!

Except, perhaps, when you'd insisted that you wanted no such intimacy in your marriage and were now regretting your hasty words.

And they had been hasty, born of the desire to control her life when those she'd trusted had proven fallible. She'd thought moving across the country would give her command over her own destiny. But the level of control she craved had proven elusive, and she was no longer sure it was even wise.

What of spontaneity? Opportunity? Adventure?
Love?

That she'd feared risking most of all. Roland's defection had hurt her, badly. Ciara and Katie Jo had tried to tell her that not every man would be so cavalier with her heart, but she hadn't been willing to listen. And yet Jesse had proven he was trustworthy, beyond what most people would have been willing to endure.

Why did trusting him seem like such a huge leap of

faith, even larger than traveling across the country to start her life over?

Jesse's mother was at the stove when Alice came downstairs. The appliance wasn't as large as the one Ciara cooked on, and it lacked the shiny appointments, but it had four burners currently covered with various pots, kettles, and pans, and the most delicious smells were coming from the oven.

"Cinnamon griddle cakes," Mrs. Willets said as if she'd noticed Alice inhaling. "I'm keeping them warm until everyone is back in the house. And that's my second batch of bacon. Ah." She smiled as Jane, Jenny, and Joanna came through the kitchen door with pails.

Alice thought she finally had the right name with the right sister. Fiery-haired Jane was the oldest, tallest, and fiercest in her actions and opinions. Jenny was next with her sleek, almost brown hair and gentle manner. And curly-haired Joanna was as likely as her brother Jeremy to tease.

"Morning, Alice," Jenny said, going to pour the creamy milk into a tall metal canister on the opposite side of the kitchen from the stove.

"Shame you missed the milking," Joanna added with a wink as she followed.

"I thought you raised cattle for beef," Alice said as Jane offered her pail to her younger sister and went to wash her hands at the big porcelain sink.

"Most are for beef," their mother clarified. "We keep a few cows for dairy—milk, butter, cheese."

Joanna licked her lips as she followed her sister to the sink. "Nothing better than butter on a slice of bread still warm from the oven."

Alice's mouth began watering.

Everyone else joined them in the kitchen and then the dining room a short while later. It turned out that Jeremy had been out half the night with the cattle, Jacob had spelled him at first light, and Jack had directed the other brothers at various chores until Alice and Jesse had come down so they could all have breakfast together.

"We heard how it is with honeymooners," Jeremy teased with a wiggle of his brows as the family passed the heaping platter of golden-brown griddle cakes around the big table after Jesse's father had said the blessing.

Alice studiously avoided looking at Jesse. "Well, I'm sorry for keeping you from this wonderful breakfast. I can hardly wait, Mrs. Willets."

"Now, I hope you'll call me Ma too," she said, handing Alice the butter dish.

"Ma two?" Jeremy said, hand to his heart. "You mean to tell me there's a Ma one?"

His mother swatted his arm. "Behave, you!"

"Always liked having good conversation at breakfast," Jesse's father said from the head of the table with a wink to Alice. "And the other meals as well."

Joy wiggled in her seat. "After breakfast, I want to show Alice the sheep. They're so sweet!"

Their father laughed. "We'll show her everything, honey."

And they did.

"And we have goats and pigs and chickens, besides cows and sheep," Joy enthused as Alice joined the cavalcade across the fields, where dozens of cows contentedly munched grass under a low-hanging sky. "We had turkeys too, but they were mean. They pecked at each other! So we ate them."

Alice may not have been raised on a farm, but she was fairly sure they ate at least the pigs as well. Still, she couldn't help smiling at the girl's excitement.

"There's something else you should see," Jesse said as they came out of the farthest of the outbuildings, which had held the pigs.

It was the first time he'd actually spoken to her since

that kiss, and she could have kicked herself for the tension between them. To show she held no hard feelings, she slipped her hand into his and beamed a smile his direction.

He started, but then a slow smile spread. He gave her hand a tug. "This way."

"Jesse's taking a girl to the drop," Jason teased, elbowing his younger brother.

Joshua rolled his eyes. "They're married. It's not the same."

"The drop?" Alice asked as they left his family behind. Now they waded through prairie grass to the north of the farm, the plants bending and snapping against her skirts.

"You'll see," Jesse said.

And all at once, she did see. Ahead, the dusky green tops of fir and the curvy tops of cedar poked up, only they reached to the middle of her chest instead of high into the sky. At the edge of the Willets' property, the land dropped steeply down, the cliffside thronged with trees and brush. Beyond them, she spotted a wide river delta, the silvery water winding and braided, until it merged with the gray of Puget Sound.

"That's the Nisqually," Jesse said, pointing. "You can't see it, but Medicine Creek runs along the bottom of the bluff. That's where Governor Stevens signed the treaty with all the tribes back in 1854." He shook his head.

She would have thought a treaty a good thing. "Was that bad?"

His gaze was off in the distance, as if he could see the convocation of tribal elders and government officials. "Some folks thought it good. It opened a lot of land to farming. But if I was a tribal member, I don't think I would have liked to be told where to live, especially when it was nowhere near where I was raised."

"But you left," Alice protested. "You came north, to Wallin Landing."

Jesse turned away from the verdant view. "I left by choice. They didn't."

Choice she understood. She had one to make about him and their future. And she needed to make it soon, for both their sakes.

The edge of the drop and the glory of the Nisqually had always filled him with awe and a sense of responsibility for protecting and nurturing what God had given. At the moment, however, Jesse wanted nothing more than to take Alice in his arms and kiss her again. His mother made gingerbread every Christmas, and each of the children had a taste from the bowl before she scraped the dough into the pan. One taste had never been enough for Jesse. One taste of Alice had merely made him want more.

Made him want forever.

But what was growing between them felt frail, tiny, like the flicker of embers as the fire started. Would he smother the flame if he put too much wood on too fast?

"So," she said as they started back for the house, "did you take other girls to see the drop?"

Jesse chuckled. "No, ma'am. You might have noticed. Marriageable gals are few and far between around here. But Jeremy and Jacob met a couple of girls at a church social in Olympia one summer and brought them out to the farm to visit."

"And that view didn't persuade them to stay?" she asked, picking up her skirts to detour around an ant hill.

Jesse put his hand to her elbow to steady her on the uneven ground, but the touch seemed to echo up his arm, whispering of hope. "No. They liked the city better."

"I thought I liked the city better," she admitted as they approached the house. "But I'm coming to love Washington Territory and Wallin Landing."

Was he a fool to hope she'd one day say she was coming to love him too?

Joy was out by the back steps, throwing grain to the chickens. She hurriedly finished and came to take Alice's other hand. "We're going to sew this morning. You should come too."

Alice glanced at Jesse, and he released his hold on her. "I'm sure you'll have fun."

She put on a smile and let Joy lead her into the house.

Jack was passing from the pasture to the barn. He tipped his head in that direction. "I could use a hand with the wagon."

Frowning, Jesse followed. "What's wrong with the wagon?"

They found Jacob on his back under the conveyance, tinkering with something.

"Brake tree's cracked," he called out. "I thought something was off when I was driving in yesterday."

Jeremy was standing with his back to a stall where they milked the cows, arms crossed over his chest. "Why does something always need to be fixed around here?"

"Because this is a working ranch," Jack said. "You work with things, they break. What do you need, Jacob?"

His younger brother shimmied out from under the wagon. "Tip it up on its side for now. Then I need a stout piece of fir or cedar we can square up to fit. And it wouldn't hurt to replace the pads while we're at it."

"You fetch the wood," Jesse said to Jeremy. "I'll shape it for you."

Jeremy looked to Jack, who nodded, then loped out of the barn.

"Give me a hand," Jack said.

Jesse braced his hands under the edge of the wagon, then leaned with his brother to ease it over onto the straw-strewn dirt floor of the barn. He couldn't help thinking about the last time he'd wrestled with a wagon, to protect Alice in the storm. He probably should have taken a chance and kept walking to Wallin Landing in the dark with her instead, but he couldn't regret his decision. He couldn't imagine Alice marrying him under any other circumstance.

"So, I guess you're in charge around here now," Jesse said as he and his brothers worked to remove the cracked brake.

Jacob made a noise, but quickly turned it into a cough.

Jack frowned at him. "Pa can't do it all anymore. Someone had to step up."

He ought to take umbrage at the words. As the oldest son, it was likely his place to take over the ranch. But he had never cottoned to it the way Jack had. Ranching seemed to run in his blood.

"Can't think of anyone better," Jesse said.

His brother's frown eased. "So, you're happy chopping trees up north?"

"For now," Jesse said, wrenching the last of the cracked wood away. "Though Alice and I are starting an apple orchard. We have the spot picked out and the seeds to plant come spring."

"An orchard," Jacob mused, stepping back as if to admire their work. "It will be needed."

Jack's gaze went out the barn door. "I wonder if we should put in a few trees."

"It's not a competition," Jacob informed him.

Once again Jack frowned. "I never said it was. But you know fruit gets mighty scarce come winter. Apples would keep in the root cellar."

"And who ever said no to a slice of apple pie?" Jeremy agreed, returning with a length of wood. He held it out to Jesse like a sword. "Your instrument, maestro."

Shaking his head at the teasing, Jesse took the piece over to the workbench along one wall.

As Jack began scraping off the old brake pad, Jacob followed Jesse to the bench.

"I never thought I'd see you with such an educated woman," he said, watching Jesse as he began planing the wood to the right thickness.

"You're not the only one with a head for information, Professor," Jeremy informed him, bringing them the block for the pad. "Or an eye for the ladies."

"As if there were any ladies to eye," Jacob grumbled.

"I think Jesse has the right of it," Jeremy said, leaning against the workbench. "Soon as I can, I'm going to advertise for a mail-order bride. I hear tell there are special circulars that distribute back East."

"And how will you know who answers?" Jacob challenged. "You may think you're corresponding with someone smart and pretty like Alice, but you might find she's the eighty-year-old tobacco-chawing granny."

Jesse let them spar, focusing on his work. He had just shaped the wood to his liking when their father came into the barn.

"What, you put him to work?" he scolded, striding over to Jesse's side. "The boy only comes home once or twice a year."

"I don't mind helping," Jesse said. He handed the brake tree to Jacob. "That work?"

"Perfect," Jacob declared.

"But then, we would expect no different," Jeremy added with a grin.

Pa took Jesse's arm. "Let's take a walk, son."

His brothers laughed, as if they thought he was in for a scolding too, but Jesse allowed his father to lead him out of the barn.

They walked toward the drop in silence a moment, and he couldn't help noticing there was a hitch in his father's gait, as if his hip was paining him.

"You all right?" Jesse asked.

His father shot him a smile. "Fit as a fiddle. But your brothers need to keep busy, so I tend to stand back and let them take the reins these days. Jeremy's been a big help with the cattle. You know how he loves to talk. Sometimes I think they listen to him better than any of the rest of us ever did. And then there's Jack." He sighed and glanced back at the barn. "That boy is determined to lead."

None of his brothers could be called boys anymore, but Jesse decided not to mention it. "Jack always liked telling everyone what to do."

His father chuckled. "He sure did. You remember that Christmas when he advised your ma what she should make for each of you?"

Jesse laughed too. "I remember the look on Jack's face when she gave him what for. But she ended up taking at least some of his suggestions."

"I see you took one of mine."

Jesse cocked his head as they reached the drop. On a good day, the Mountain stood at the head of the valley, tall and proud, and the Olympics sparkled across the Sound as if waving hello to their larger cousin.

"I always try to take your suggestions, Pa," he said.

"I know you do." His father patted his shoulder. "I'm just glad you found a gal you could love who'd love you back."

Guilt smacked him harder than a widow maker. "Well, it isn't exactly like that with me and Alice."

His father's smile faded. "What do you mean?"

Jesse wasn't sure what he said afterward. Jeremy and Ma had always been the talkers in the family, but now his words just kept coming, about the storm, about Gladys Volland and her ultimatum, about Alice standing there small and scared looking. And then the request for a marriage of convenience, the wedding, the story of why Alice left Cawthorn, the cabin raising, the two sleeping rooms, and Roland Cawthorn showing up as if he intended to take Alice away.

"And then she kissed me," he finished. "This morning, when we were waking up. Truly, Pa, I don't know whether I'm coming or going."

His father patted his shoulder again. "Sounds like you're in the middle of a courtship with your own wife. Some courtships are up and down and every way in between before they're settled to everyone's satisfaction."

Jesse scrunched up his face. "Really?"

"Really," his father assured him. "Take it slow and easy. Sounds like that Cawthorn fellow disappointed her real bad. Show her you're a man who can be trusted. Why, I courted your mother for months before she even noticed!"

Jesse stared at him. "I thought it was love at first sight with you and Ma."

His father winked. "I was in love at first sight. Your ma took some convincing. And look at us now. You could be in the same place in twenty years, son."

Now, there was a dream worth pursuing.

CHAPTER SIXTEEN

JESSE'S MOTHER AND sisters had set up their sewing circle in the parlor. Ma Willets and Joanna shared the sofa, though Joanna slid over to make room for her littlest sister as Joy led in Alice. Jane and Jenny sat on two of the ladder-back chairs. Jane nodded Alice into a third nearby. On the side table, a wooden caddy held spools of thread of every color and a calico pin cushion shaped like a pumpkin bristled with needles. She caught the scent of lavender as she sat.

Each of the ladies was working on white fabric about a foot square, studiously embroidering what appeared to be wreaths and bouquets of flowers.

"What are you making?" Alice asked as Jenny offered her a square of fabric for herself. Someone had lightly marked off a large heart in the center with pencil.

"A quilt," Joy declared.

"A special quilt," Joanna agreed, pulling up her thread. "For a special couple."

"Oh?" Alice asked, looking for scarlet thread for the heart. "Is someone getting married?"

Joy giggled.

Alice glanced up to find them all beaming at her.

"We wanted to make a quilt for you and Jesse, dear," Ma said. "There wasn't time to finish it before you arrived, but we hope to have it done when you come again." She cocked her head. "Perhaps at Christmas?"

Alice's throat felt tight. "I'd like that. And thank you all so much!"

Joy popped out of her seat to venture closer. "It's a flower quilt with baskets and wreaths and bouquets, and there's a big heart in the middle." She pointed to Alice's piece. "That shows how much you love each other."

If only that were true! "It sounds wonderful," Alice managed.

Joy swished her skirts back and forth. "I'm making a bouquet." She leaned closer. "Ma says that's a fancy name for a bunch of flowers."

Alice smiled despite her misgivings. "What color are your flowers?"

"Blue and red and yellow," Joy answered. "And purple. I like purple."

"I like it better when you finish your work," her mother said.

Joy ducked her head and hurried back to her seat.

"Tell us about your school, Alice," Ma requested.

And so she told them about her eight precious students, what they liked, how they acted, and her hopes for them. In turn, they told her about their family, the good times and the bad. She loved hearing the stories, but she began to see one of the reasons why her husband was so quiet. When would he have had a moment to talk!

Finally, their mother set her square aside and rose. "I need to check on the roast. Alice, would you help me?"

The other girls exchanged glances, but no one said a word as Alice followed Jesse's mother out.

Ma gave her arm a squeeze. "I just wanted a chat with you. You have the keeping of my firstborn son. That's a big responsibility. How are you holding up?"

"Fine," Alice said brightly as they came into the kitchen. "Your Jesse is a dear."

"Your Jesse now." His mother took a corner of her apron to protect her hand and opened the door of the oven. Savory scents danced on the air.

"Coming along nicely," she proclaimed as she shut the door and straightened. "He looks sad. Are they working him too hard?"

"No," Alice assured her. "That is, he works hard, but he seems to take pride in it." She paused for a moment. "You think he looks sad?"

"Yes, I do." She leaned a hip on the sideboard. "Jesse was never one to talk and talk. He keeps things close. But you can see his feelings in his eyes. He looks at you, and he looks sad."

Guilt wrapped its arms about her. "I'm so sorry."

Ma raised her brows. "Do you have a reason to apologize?"

"Yes, no, that is." Alice drew in a deep breath and said a prayer for the words to explain. "You see, Jesse and I didn't marry for love. We had to spend the night together because of a storm, and the schoolboard president decided that ruined my reputation. So it was either marry or lose my position. Jesse offered to marry me."

"Of course he did," his mother muttered before raising her voice. "And you? Did you find nothing admirable about my son?"

She couldn't bristle at the tone. If she ever had a son, she'd likely feel the same way if he'd ended up in this situation.

"I find many things admirable about Jesse," she told his mother. "He's kind. He's generous with his time and talents, to the point that he sometimes overlooks his own needs. He's loyal and thoughtful and sweet-natured. And I'm afraid I'm falling in love with him."

Ma rocked back. "Well."

Alice nodded. "But I'm not sure how to tell him. I'm the one who insisted on a marriage of convenience. And he's likely to agree to something more just to be helpful! I couldn't bear that."

Ma straightened and came to enfold her in a hug. "You're right. But did you ever wonder if Jesse looks sad because he's hoping for something more too? The only way to know is to ask."

To take a chance that he would prove as steadfast and true as he seemed. After meeting his family, seeing how he was raised, how could she believe he'd be anything less?

Ma released her with a watery smile. "Just keep your heart and mind open, Alice. You might be surprised by the good that comes of it. Why I had to flutter my lashes and giggle at Jesse's father for months before he got up the nerve to talk to me."

Alice blinked. "Why, I thought you and Mr. Willets fell in love at first sight."

"Well, *I* did," Ma said. "But it took him a while to get used to the idea. I think Jesse's already halfway there."

She certainly was.

She didn't see him again until just before dinner, and then there was no time for a private conversation. She took a few bites of his mother's delectable roast and only attended to half the conversation around her at the table and in the parlor later, intent on crafting her speech in her mind. Her stomach was fluttering as she and Jesse climbed the stairs to the bedrooms.

But as soon as she reached the top, she found Joanna, Joy, Jenny, and Jane waiting.

"Our turn," Joanna proclaimed, latching onto Alice's arm. "You're going to sleep with us tonight, Alice."

"What?" Alice asked, glancing among them and seeing only grins.

Joy was bouncing on her feet. "We're all going to sleep in one room and tell stories!"

"Alice?" Jesse asked with a frown.

"Well, I," Alice began.

"You get her all the time, Jesse," Jane informed him, hand on one hip. "We only have tonight. We'll see you in the morning."

"But my nightgown," Alice protested.

"Already moved to our room," Jenny assured her. "Good night, Jesse."

Jesse nodded, but Alice could see his face, and she could only agree with his mother that he looked sad.

Much as she missed Jesse, Alice had to own that the night with his sisters was fun. Her parents hadn't seen the need for her to spend much time with other children outside of school, unless they were the children of those who were more prominent socially, like Roland. She might take tea at a friend's house or work on a charitable project together, but those interactions paled in comparison to the companionship of Jesse's sisters.

"So, how did you and Jesse meet?" Joanna wanted to know. Alice had been given one of the beds. Jenny and Joy were sharing the other, and Joanna and Jane had spread blankets on the floor, like Jesse had had to do when he and Alice had been living in her quarters.

"Jesse brought me in from the steamer to Wallin Landing," Alice explained. "But he didn't say a lot, so I wasn't sure of him. Mr. Drew Wallin, his employer, pays my friend, Ciara Weatherly, to cook for his men and me, as the schoolteacher. That meant Jesse and I saw each other most breakfasts and dinners."

"And you noticed he was tall and strong," Jenny said dreamily, and Alice could imagine her blue eyes misty. "With the nicest smile."

"I did," Alice said, vowing not to tell them she'd also feared he was rather dim at first.

"And he saw you were pretty and sweet," Joy put in.

She wasn't entirely sure what Jesse had first noticed about her, but she decided to turn the tables on them. "And what about you? Jesse tells me there are few young ladies in the area and lots of gentlemen, which means you can have your pick!"

"If you want men who spend their days covered in sawdust and their nights at the saloon," Jane said, and the bedclothes rustled as if her tall frame had shuddered. "I can admire a man who works hard, but not one who wastes his money on alcohol and…" She seemed to recall her little sister, likely listening avidly. "Other things," she finished.

"What other things?" Joy asked.

"Macassar oil for his hair," Jenny offered, and she must have tickled her sister, for Joy giggled.

"Oh, some men wore that in Cawthorn, where I'm from," Alice told them. "I never liked it. It smelled like jasmine, but it made their hair far too shiny."

"Like a greased pig," Joanna suggested, and now they all laughed.

"I'm not sure I'd like to marry a man who smelled better than I did," Jane said.

"Alice doesn't have to worry about that with Jesse," Joanna teased.

"Your brother smells just fine," Alice protested, and they laughed some more. She was glad they couldn't see her cheeks turning red in the dark.

"I think finding a fellow to love must be easier for you, Alice," Jane said. "I've had one or two approach me at our church meetings, but they keep eyeing me funny."

"Some men don't like a lady to be taller than them," Jenny explained.

"Oh, surely not," Alice protested.

"Surely so," Jane said. "I even had one suggest I should hunch over, so I didn't tower over him."

"Worse are the ones who complain about too much ginger on top, as if I were a cookie," Jenny said indignantly.

"Well, they clearly have no concept of their own consequence," Alice said. "I quite agree with your brother, Jacob. Beauty comes from within, and you are all truly beautiful."

A pillow sailed across the room and bounced off her stomach.

"Yes, we are!" Joanna declared. "Who needs a man anyway?"

Her sisters all made hear, hear noises, but Alice thought at least Jane's sounded wistful.

They finally fell asleep, but Alice was yawning as she came downstairs the next morning, barely covering her mouth in time as she entered the kitchen.

"Those girls," Ma said with a shake of her head. "I heard they carried you off last night, Alice. You should have told them to leave you be."

"I didn't mind," Alice said, stepping forward to help her with a platter of toast she was balancing. "Jane, Jenny, Joanna, and Joy are dears. And so are you." She pressed a kiss to the lady's cheek.

Ma smiled at her. "You as well, darling girl. I'll be praying for you."

In fact, she and Jesse's father prayed over them before Alice and Jesse left for the dock. Alice kept looking back as Jack drove the wagon out onto the main road. This was the sort of family she wanted—one that teased and laughed and loved and cared through good times and bad. She linked her arm with Jesse's and smiled up at him.

"Your mother wants us to come back for Christmas," she said. "Could we?"

He lay his hand over hers. "Sure."

Jack laughed. "My brother, the man of few words."

Alice regarded him. "Sometimes, sir, only a few words are necessary and the rest is extraneous."

Jack sat taller. "Yes, ma'am."

Now Jesse laughed.

She didn't have a moment to speak with him in private until they'd boarded the *Northern Star* and were steaming out into the Sound to the tune of the *Star Spangled Banner* this time. Now that she knew what to look for, she easily spotted the wide delta of the Nisqually and the forested hillside that led up to the Willets' farm.

"They might be watching us even now," she said with a nod to the bluff as she and Jesse stood on the deck, the planks vibrating under their feet. "I truly enjoyed meeting your family. I suppose I should say our family now."

He glanced her way. "They'd be happy to hear you claim kinship."

She braced both hands on the rail, gripping the wood, which was as firm as her conviction. Now was the time. This was the place. Yet her carefully rehearsed speech seemed to have evaporated. Was Jesse's quiet contagious?

She forced a breath and dove in. "Your mother and father are clearly devoted to each other. Was that what you expected from your own marriage?"

"Yes."

She turned to face him. "Then we should talk, Jesse. Really talk. Using more than one-syllable words. Because I'm starting to think that's what I want too."

She looked so earnest, so determined. After spending time with his sisters and mother, he shouldn't be surprised.

"We can talk," he said and added a silent prayer that God would give him the words. "What sort of marriage did *you* want growing up?"

Her gaze went off across the white caps. "It was different in my family. There was respect and, I suppose, love, but it wasn't expressed the way your family expresses it. We didn't hug in public and rarely even in private. It was all expressed in words. I suppose that's what I expected from a husband."

Words. Words with more than one syllable. Words that he worked so hard to find. "I can try to use more words."

Her gaze came back to him. "But don't you see, Jesse? I'm coming to realize there's more than words."

"What did you have in mind?" he asked, fearing to hope.

Her fingers left the rail to wrap around each other. "A marriage where we dream together, make decisions together."

Jesse nodded. "Sort of thought we were doing that now."

Her smile was soft. "Like with the orchard. Yes. But it's more than that. I want a marriage where we truly care for each other, emotionally and physically." She looked at him, then quickly away, and her cheeks were turning redder than the cold warranted.

Part of him wanted to leave it be at that, but he needed to know. "Where we share the same bed?"

She dropped her gaze to the deck. "Yes."

Such a small word, holding depths of fear and longing. Jesse lay his hand over hers. "I'd like that, but only if you're sure."

"Oh, Jesse." She came into his arms and laid her head on his chest, and he held her. Against the wind, against the fear, against whatever lay in their future. She was his. And he would never take that for granted.

He could have held her forever, but she started to shiver, and he was pretty sure even *her* words were failing her. So he led her back into the cabin. A few other passengers were already gathered around the stove, and he was thankful none were smoking. But he and Alice had no opportunity to do more than exchange smiles. And

Harry was waiting at the dock in Seattle, which meant they couldn't do much more than that there either.

So, he let Alice and Harry talk about what had been going on at the Landing since they'd left, and Jesse stretched his legs in the bed of the wagon and dreamed about having a marriage with Alice at his side, day and night.

"I just want to make sure the schoolroom is ready for tomorrow," she said when they reached the Landing. "I'll only be a minute, Jesse."

He nodded, and she lifted her skirts to hurry for the school. Jesse grabbed the valise out of the wagon, turned, and found Harry blocking his way.

"I didn't want to say anything in front of Alice," his friend said. "But you need to know something. That Cawthorn fellow didn't leave. He's still staying at the inn. Claims he has more to say to Alice."

Over his dead body.

CHAPTER SEVENTEEN

"WHERE IS HE?" Jesse demanded.

Harry grinned. "Probably sitting in his room. Want me to fetch him for you?"

Jesse nodded.

He followed Harry into the inn. It was late enough in the day that the tables had been set for the dinner service, though Ciara had yet to turn the sign to Open. The air smelled of fresh-baked bread. Little Grace toddled up to grab Jesse's trousers. Much as he wanted to look stern for his confrontation with Cawthorn, he couldn't help smiling down at her.

"Think you're smart, don't you?"

"No, no, no, no, no," Grace said.

Jesse bent and scooped her up into his arms. "Well, I'll have to disagree with you there." He tossed her into the air and caught her, and she laughed.

Ciara came out of the kitchen. "*There* she is! I swear that girl walks farther faster every day. Thank you, Jesse, for keeping her safe."

"My pleasure." He handed the baby to Ciara.

Grace wiggled her fingers at him. "Again."

"Oh, a new word," Jesse said. "See, I told you that you were smart."

"Yes, she is a delightful child," drawled a voice.

They both turned to find Roland Cawthorn coming

down the stairs with Harry. Alice's former suitor was a dandy if ever Jesse had seen one—hair all shiny with pomade, coat so tailored to his frame he likely couldn't swing an ax if he tried.

As if she suspected what was about to happen, Ciara carried Grace back to the safety of the kitchen. The baby waved at Jesse over her shoulder.

"What a way you have with the ladies, Mr. Willets," Cawthorn said.

"You need any help, Jesse?" Harry asked, cracking a knuckle.

"No." He nodded as Harry sauntered into the kitchen after Ciara. Likely his friend should be heading to his own claim, where Katie Jo would be waiting if she wasn't helping at the inn tonight. He was staying to give Jesse his support.

Jesse widened his stance and focused on the newcomer. "I hear you want to have words with my wife."

He'd meant to look determined, but those last two words forced him to smile. Whatever this fellow did, Alice was Jesse's wife, and there was nothing Cawthorn could do about it.

Or so he had thought.

"Can we sit?" Cawthorn motioned to the smallest table near the stairs.

He would have preferred to have it out right here, but Ciara would likely need to open the restaurant at any moment. She wouldn't thank him for putting her customers in the position of watching two roosters peck at each other. So, Jesse sat.

Cawthorn steepled his fingers. "I care a great deal about Alice. I only want to see her happy."

"You should have thought of her happiness before you fixed on another gal," Jesse said.

He winced, lowering his hands. "I see she's shared that sorry tale. What can I say? I was an idiot."

Jesse crossed his arms over his chest. "You won't see me arguing."

As if he were used to people rushing to assure him of his worth, his face darkened, but he pressed on. "Alice inspires the best in those around her. I can see you care about her, and she seems to have grown fond of you."

Immediately, doubts began poking. *What, Jesse? Did you think she could love you? She grew up believing men with words made the best husbands. Men like this one.*

"But I can give her so much more," Cawthorn continued as if he knew Jesse was weakening. "A proper house with indoor plumbing, tickets to the theatre and opera, friends to cheer and guide. She must miss her family terribly. They certainly miss her."

"We're married," Jesse blurted. "Nothing to be done about that."

"Isn't there?" He eyed Jesse a moment, then leaned closer. "You may have fooled the others, but I know better. I visited your hovel while you were gone. You really should employ a lock. What I found surprised me. You have two beds, both of which appear to be in use. Admit it—you haven't consummated the marriage. Alice doesn't love you. Your vows are a sham."

Jesse surged to his feet, blood roaring. "You had no right."

He rose more slowly. "I had every right. I love Alice. If you love her, you'd know sending her back to Cawthorn is best for her. She can never be happy here. I understand all you have to do is petition the Territorial Legislature, and you can do that even if Alice is living in another state. Let me take Alice home."

His breath burned in his chest. His hands fisted. He wanted to shove that smug smile down Roland Cawthorn's throat and throw him out of the inn, out of the settlement. But he stood a good six inches taller than the fellow and likely outweighed him by twenty pounds or more. It wouldn't be fair.

And it wasn't fair to Alice to keep this decision from her. The people she'd loved had tried to decide her life before. This was her choice.

With a pang, he realized he'd gone and done it. He'd tumbled into love with his own wife, and he wanted her to be happy, truly happy. Even if that meant letting her go.

"I'll talk to her," he gritted out. "It's Alice's decision to make, not mine."

He strode out of the inn for the school. He was either about to make his marriage.

Or end it.

Alice gazed around her classroom. Whoever had managed it while she had been gone had done an excellent job. The chalkboard was wiped clean, the floor swept. She had only to center her chair behind her desk. Her school. Her community.

Her husband.

The last was so amazing she pressed both fingers to her lips. Jesse was willing to be her husband, in every sense of that word. She wanted to float about the room like a balloon set free. Yes, she was a little nervous about what being a wife entailed, but every bride might be expected to feel the same way.

Her. A bride. It didn't matter that she had married him two weeks ago now. Today, she was truly a bride. Somewhere along the line she had fallen in love with her husband, and she knew it was a true love, the kind her parents might scoff at but the Bible talked about.

Love suffereth long and is kind. Love envieth not. Love vaunteth not itself, is not puffed up, doth not behave itself unseemly, seeketh not its own, is not easily provoked, thinketh no evil, rejoiceth not in iniquity but rejoiceth in truth. Love beareth all things, believeth all things, hopeth all things.

They had a ways to go to truly understand each other, but that, that was the kind of love she and Jesse might grow into. It was enough to make a lady giddy!

The thump of a footstep made her turn to beam upon her husband.

But Jesse didn't smile back. He was pale as he ambled toward her.

Alice hurried to meet him and set a hand on his arm. "Jesse! What is it? What's happened?"

"We need to talk," he said.

She almost laughed, never at him but at the silliness of it all. Her dear, sweet, tongue-tied husband wanted to talk. Of course he looked worried about it.

She took his hand and led him over to her desk, then pushed on his shoulders to have him sit in her chair. "There. That's better. What would you like to talk about?"

He ran a hand back through his hair. "Roland Cawthorn still wants to marry you."

This time she did laugh. "Well, poor Roland Cawthorn. I'm already married."

"Not really." He rubbed a toe against the wood of the floor, the squeak audible in the quiet classroom. "He's the sort of feller you wanted to marry, Alice, cultured and smart."

"If he was all that smart, he wouldn't have kept me dangling for years only to throw me over," Alice said primly.

"He says he's sorry for that."

"I doubt he means it."

He shrugged. "He sounded like he means it."

"And he sounded as if he truly cared about me, until he didn't." She reached out to take one of his hands. "I don't want to go back to Cawthorn, Jesse."

"You sure?" His head came up, and his gaze was

tortured. "Because if that would make you happy, Alice, I would be willing to give you a divorce. I love you."

Her breath caught, and she pressed her other hand to her mouth again.

"It's true," he said, as if he thought she doubted him. "I love you. Maybe I really am dim that it took me this long to figure it out. But I love you, Alice, and I want the best for you."

"Oh, Jesse." She wrapped her arms about his shoulders. "*I'm* the one who's been dim. I fussed at you, and I tried to correct you, when I simply wasn't seeing you. Now I see you, and you're glorious!"

He frowned. "Me?"

"You," she promised him, giving him a squeeze. "I don't need to go back to Cawthorn with Roland to be happy. I have everything I ever wanted right here, including the love of a fine man. I know it's in your very nature to help people, but don't help me this time, Jesse. Fight for me! Because I love you too!"

Up he came, knocking her arms aside then pulling her into his embrace. This was no tentative kiss. It demanded a response she rejoiced to give. She kissed him back, long and deep. When they finally leaned back, neither was breathing properly.

"I'm never letting you go," he promised.

"Good," Alice said. "And please don't listen to anything else Roland might say. We are not going to let the Cawthorns take something else fine and good and squeeze the life from it."

"Yes, ma'am."

She had to kiss him again. And again. Until he wore the most fatuous smile on his handsome face.

"I'm going to tell Cawthorn a thing or two," he said. "You want to wait at the cabin?"

Alice smiled. "Oh, no. I wouldn't miss this for the world."

Alice loved him. That was all Jesse needed to know to stand his ground. He cradled her hand in his as the two of them crossed the clearing. He'd only seen the Abolitionists protest in the Territorial capital once, but they hadn't marched as proudly as Alice did. She was sure in her decision about staying in Wallin Landing and becoming his wife. He was truly blessed.

Ciara had started serving dinner when they entered. Already miners and farmers filled the seats, with a line forming at the door. Cawthorn was at the same small table, dipping his spoon in the venison stew Ciara had cooked that night. Dixon Hitchcock and Kit were having dinner at another table with Grace. She waved to Jesse, but he could barely spare her a smile before focusing on the man who had broken his Alice's heart.

"No," he said.

Cawthorn settled back in his seat. "Odd. I was assured that that was what babies say around here."

Heat flushed up him. "And here I thought you were a smart fellow." He leaned closer. "No, Alice is not returning back East with you. She's happy here, as my wife. Feel free to leave any time, and don't come back."

Alice snapped a nod as if to prove as much.

Cawthorn rested his hands on his belly. "I highly doubt that Alice is truly happy. In fact, I begin to believe she's being taken advantage of. I will be speaking to an attorney on her behalf."

"What!" Alice glared at him. "You have no right to speak to anyone on my behalf!"

"Your family would expect it of me," he said with so much complacency that Jesse's hand fisted anew.

"He may be right."

Jesse turned to find Hitchcock at their side. As if he knew Jesse was at the end of his rope, the lawyer lay a hand on his shoulder, then inclined his head to Alice. "Forgive the interruption, Mr. and Mrs. Willets, but I believe I can shed a little light on this subject. At your husband's request, I asked some friends to look into why a gentleman like Mr. Cawthorn would come all this way and remain in our fair town so long."

Cawthorn threw down his napkin and rose. "How dare you poke your nose into my personal affairs! I demand your name, sir."

Hitchcock patted Jesse's shoulder before releasing him and offering Cawthorn a little bow. "Dixon Hitchcock, attorney and friend to Mr. and Mrs. Willets." He immediately straightened and refocused on Alice, who was frowning. "It seems you felt pressured into fleeing your home because of this fellow, Mrs. Willets, and that you are under the impression that your family blames you for his defection."

Alice paled. "I was told as much. Repeatedly."

Jesse could feel her pain. So could Hitchcock, it seemed, for his smile was kind. "Well, they appear to have had a change of heart. Your leaving greatly distressed your brother and parents as well as your friends, not to mention Mr. Cawthorn's parents. The entire town ordered him to seek you out, apologize, and return you to their bosoms."

Alice stared at her former suitor. "Is this true, Roland?"

"You have a more loyal following than you know," he said stiffly. "I have been told repeatedly that it is entirely my fault you left."

"Good," Jesse said with a nod, which only stiffened his back further.

Alice narrowed her eyes. "And what does Miss Holladay have to say about this?"

His gaze did not meet hers. "Miss Holladay decided we would not suit."

So, he'd been served as he'd served Alice. There was a justice in that.

"A shame," Alice said. "But I fail to see why I should trouble myself on your behalf."

"On the behalf of your parents and Gerald," he insisted. "It is my duty to bring you home."

She latched onto Jesse's arm as if to anchor herself beside him. "I *am* home."

Jesse had to stop himself from crowing in triumph.

Cawthorn's mouth thinned. "If you have any tender feelings left for your family, I suggest you pack your things and come with me, before it's too late."

He just didn't understand. Jesse shook his head. "You still think you can bully her into going with you." He bent and put his face into Cawthorn's. "That isn't going to happen. She's happy here."

"Happy!" Cawthorn spat out the word, but he managed to take a step back from Jesse. "How can she be happy? She's teaching children with whom her family would never have allowed her to associate." He waved at Ciara's fine stew. "She's eating slop. And she's been forced to live in the dirt, her lodging no better than a pigsty."

Jesse drew himself up, but Alice moved in front of him. "Allow me, darling."

Darling. He was grinning as she turned to Cawthorn.

"How dare you insult my home, you pusillanimous reprobate! I'll have you know I helped construct that establishment. And I am honored to instruct my students. They are far more intelligent and diligent than you could imagine. Furthermore, Ciara's cooking would rival that of a master of cuisine at the finest restaurant in Boston. However, if you require proper elocution to convince you of my intentions, I would be delighted to educate you further."

She raised her chin and drilled her gaze into him. Jesse almost pitied the fellow.

"You could perambulate across our venerable republic and fail to stumble upon a finer example of community, camaraderie, and compassion than exists here at Wallin Landing. I could extol the flora and fauna, mountainous crags, silvery rills, and verdant valleys that surround us. I could enumerate the many outstanding examples of ferocity, farsightedness, and fortitude I have been privileged to witness from these stalwart citizens. And you think you can utter a few simple words to persuade me otherwise?"

She took a step forward, and Cawthorn flinched. "You, sir," she spit out, "are a scurrilous, sanctimonious sensationalist to slander our sacred institutions." She pointed at the door. "*You* gather your things and leave this instant, or I will press charges against you for harassment, trespassing, and defamation of character."

Chaos resulted. Half the diners applauded, and the other half stomped their booted feet in appreciation, setting the log rafters to rattling. A few whistled long and loud, so that Jesse barely heard Hitchcock say, "And I would be delighted to prosecute the case for you, dear lady."

Cawthorn had his back pressed to the wall, eyes wide and face flushed. Before he could say another word, two of the miners rose and shoved forward.

"You want us to run him out of town on a rail, Mrs. Willets?" one asked, eyes narrowed as if he'd spotted a fox in the hen house.

"Tar and feather him?" the other offered, grin positively eager.

"I'd be happy to heat the tar myself," Logan Bradshaw offered from another table, and his boy nodded.

Alice looked to Jesse. "No, that shouldn't be necessary, gentlemen, though I appreciate your thoughtfulness. If Mr. Cawthorn cannot find his own way to the door, I'm sure my husband can help him."

Cawthorn took one look at Jesse and bolted up the stairs.

More applause thundered.

Alice spread her skirts in a curtsey before latching onto Jesse's arm anew. The touch spoke of conviction, of care. Of courage to face the future, together. "Let's go home, Jesse."

CHAPTER EIGHTEEN

Two weeks later

"SO, I BELIEVE we are agreed," Alice said, glancing around at the four members of the Committee to Study the Incorporation of the Community Called Wallin Landing.

Drew Wallin was nodding. Dawes Cooper was leaning back in his seat, lower lip out thoughtfully. Winston Merganser had his fingers laced over his belly, and Ciara was grinning at her. The only one missing was Gladys Volland. Her husband had recently sold their farm and moved them south, claiming the need for a drier climate. No one had shed a tear over that.

And no one had shed a tear over Roland Cawthorn's departure either. It was clear to Alice that he'd only come to Wallin Landing because he hadn't been able to stand the thought of appearing less in the eyes of the citizens of Cawthorn. He never had cared anything about her. He'd fled to Seattle that very evening she and Jesse had confronted him, and they had heard he'd taken a ship south to catch a train back East. Alice had followed to Seattle on Saturday to telegraph her parents, assure them she was happy, and encourage them to come visit if they liked.

They had since written back their hopes for her future, but they had declined to make any promises about coming this way. It was just as well. As much as she loved her parents and their defense of her in the end, they were still far too used to bowing and scraping to the mighty Cawthorns. What Wallin Landing needed were visionaries like the ones seated around her desk.

Alice studied her notes. "We will propose following the model of Port Townsend. Wallin Landing would be overseen by a five-member Board of Trustees elected annually and serving on a volunteer basis. We would assess a minimal tax by claim or household to hire a Town Clerk who would manage the day-to-day affairs and a Town Marshall for public safety."

Drew glanced around as well. "All in favor?"

Ayes rumbled against the walls of the schoolroom.

"Opposed?" He waited.

"You didn't really have to ask that," Mr. Merganser put in. "We all said yes."

"Mr. Wallin is following appropriate conduct for a committee meeting," Alice informed him. "And I thank him for that, just as I commend you all for your insightful deliberations. It will be noted in the minutes that the committee's vote was unanimous."

"And that's enough for today," Drew said. "We'll get together next week to discuss how we connect the school administration to the structure we're proposing. Meeting adjourned."

One by one, they rose and left, nodding their thanks to Alice on the way out. Ciara winked at her before going through the door.

Only Drew remained behind. "Fine work, Alice. Thank you."

"It's a pleasure to help such a worthwhile endeavor," she told him, tidying her papers. "I'll copy this in triplicate so it can be submitted to the territory, filed with the committee papers, and kept with the historical papers of the settlement."

He chuckled. "You assume we have historical papers."

Alice cocked her head. "Why, certainly you should. I'll speak with your brother John. I'm sure between the two of us we can document the beginnings."

"You might be able to at that." He turned to go, then looked back. "I'm very glad the schoolboard hired you. You were just what this settlement needed."

Pleasure rippled through her as he went out the door. And it only doubled when she spotted Jesse coming in after him.

"All done?" he asked.

Alice gathered her things. "For today. Let's go home. Ciara showed me how to make apple and pork pie, and I'd love to try it. We have all the ingredients."

He licked his lips. "Sounds good to me."

They exited the schoolhouse, and she took his arm. An arm she could lean on in the bad times, an arm that held her so gently in the good times. Her convenient marriage had turned into something she had never thought possible.

A marriage of true love.

They walked through the misty woods to the cabin, the toot of a willow bark whistle sounding in the distance. Jesse opened the door for her. They were all moved in now and using only one of the bedrooms. The other, she knew, was reserved for their children.

"Ma wrote," Jesse said, going for the bucket while she bent over the hearth. She knew how to lay and start the fire now, and how to keep it going. She'd learned so much since coming to Wallin Landing.

"How is everyone?" she asked, striking the flint over the tinder she'd set out before going to the meeting.

"Good," he said, heading for the door and the pump

outside. "She was glad to hear we intend to come for Christmas."

Alice smiled as she watched the little dry sticks catch and glow. "I should have a week off from school."

She busied herself with tending the fire, but her mind kept humming. Would she have time to make or buy presents for his siblings? No, she should give them books! They had all sounded so eager to learn. Jesse would know what they already had. Surely between the ones she'd brought with her and what Seattle had to offer, she could find something new to interest them.

He came back in and set the bucket on the table, then nodded to her work. "You're getting good at that."

Alice smiled, straightening. "And I hope to prove I'm getting better at cooking too. I'm trying to copy what I saw your mother do, even though we don't have a stove yet."

"A few more months," he promised, "and we can place the order." She watched as he rolled up his sleeves and dipped his hands in the cool water. Moisture beaded on muscle.

"You know I admire your parents in all ways," she said, rising. "They are a pattern card for a marriage."

He grinned as she came up to him. "They sure are."

Alice slipped her hands about his waist. "I think we should copy them in another way too."

"How so?"

Alice fluttered her lashes. "Ten children, perhaps?"

His smile broadened. "Happy to help, Mrs. Willets."

Thank you for choosing Alice and Jesse's story. I so enjoyed helping them find the love that lay in plain sight. If you missed how Alice came to Wallin Landing, be sure to read *Frontier Cinderella*, which tells the story of Katie Jo and Harry's bumpy courtship. *Would-Be Wilderness Wife* tells how young Mercer Belle Catherine Stanway came to Wallin Landing and married Drew. You can find all the books in the Frontier Matches (and the Frontier Bachelors series that preceded them) listed on my website at *https://www.reginascott.com/frontierbachelors.html.*

Did you enjoy meeting Jesse's family? His brothers and sisters deserve happily ever afters too. Turn the page for a sneak peek at the first book in their series, Frontier Brides, *Sudden Mail-Order Bride.* Jeremy Willets has a lot of explaining to do when the young lady with whom he's been secretly corresponding shows up at the door, in a heap of trouble.

SNEAK PEEK:

SUDDEN MAIL-ORDER BRIDE

REGINA SCOTT

CHAPTER ONE

Near Olympia, Washington Territory
March 1877

IF SHE HAD to marry a stranger, she'd picked a pretty place to do it.

Caroline Cadhill peered out from the bed of the wagon that was bumping along a muddy road in the middle of nowhere. After leaving Olympia, she'd lost all sense of direction. The sun was masked by puffy white clouds, so she couldn't even be sure of the shadows. But she was fairly sure those larger white things on the horizon weren't clouds. They were mountains.

Real, snowy mountains!

She shivered, but more from excitement. *Ready or not, Jeremy Willets, here I come!*

The farmer who had been recommended to her to take her the last leg of her long journey called to his horses and drew them to a stop beside a drive that opened to one side of the road. "Here you go, miss. This is the Willets ranch."

He made no move to help her down, but she was used to such things now. Ever since Papa had been convicted of a crime she still couldn't believe he'd committed, everyone she'd known in Cincinnati had kept their distance, as if she'd contracted consumption. And on the way West, most folks had been too focused on their own affairs to pay a stranger much mind.

So, she scooted to the open end of the buckboard, dragging her valise with her. "Thank you very much for the ride, Mr. Abercromby. I hope to see you around."

He grunted. Likely he wondered whether she was going to be staying more than a few minutes.

She wondered the same.

She shinnied off the end of the wagon, then arranged her gingham skirts about her. She'd barely had time to lower the bag before he clucked to the horses and rattled off down the road. Putting one hand to her bonnet to straighten it, she picked up the battered leather valise with the other and started down the drive.

All around her, grasses bright with the green of spring waved in a gentle breeze. Roan cattle raised their heads, chewing contentedly, to watch her pass. To their backs rose the solid, dusky green of a forest, its depths shadowed and mysterious. The air smelled clean, as if freshly washed.

You're a long way from home, Caro.

And wasn't that the point? No more attending society events pretending that she hadn't lost everything and being pitied and shunned anyway. No more living along dusty streets where men shambled about begging for a penny for bread. No more fearing she might not have enough money for bread for herself and Ned.

As always, the thought of her brother raised emotions, both sad and confused. Why had he left without telling her? Where was he now? Was he safe? Fed?

Please, Lord, keep Your hand on him and give me strength to follow this path.

Ahead, a white clapboard two-story house came into view, twin barns rising behind it. The wide porch crossed the front, with chairs here and there under the windows as if to encourage lingering with a book and a cup of tea.

The two young red-headed women out in the yard seemed far more industrious than the porch implied. Aprons covering much of their gingham dresses, they were hanging clothes on a line that stretched from one porch pole to a pole in the middle of the yard.

Jane? Jenny? Joanna? Joy would surely be smaller. Caroline's steps quickened.

"I have a large family," he'd written to her after she'd first emboldened herself to answer his ad for a mail-order bride. "Four sisters and five brothers, although the oldest brother lives north of us quite a distance. There may not be a town near the ranch, but we've never lacked for good society."

That was one of the things she'd admired about Jeremy. He knew how to turn a phrase. And over the course of the next three months, as they'd corresponded, she'd learned all about his siblings, from their ages and descriptions to their personalities. She'd thought she'd also learned something of the man in the process.

He preferred to find the laughter in troubles instead of hanging onto the pain. She had the same philosophy,

He looked for the easiest, quickest ways of doing things, which she had to remind herself to do.

"Some might call that laziness," he'd written. "I see it more as efficiency. You could spend hours tilling, planting, and harvesting your own hay for the winter feeding of the cattle, but why not buy some from the farmer down the road, who will thank you for helping his family?"

And that came through most of all. Jeremy Willets cared deeply about family. He might tease and joke about his, but it was clear he'd do just about anything to make them smile. She suspected that was the reason he hadn't sent for her yet. He wasn't convinced she would fit.

She hadn't truly fit in Cincinnati. She had no real expectation of fitting in here, though wouldn't it be nice if she did? What she really needed was somewhere safe to stay for a while. Surely he'd agree to that, even if he had decided not to marry her.

The taller young lady noticed her first, and my, was she tall! Caroline would have put her at least six inches above her own five and a half feet height. She had managed to tame her hair back into a bun at the nape of her neck, but that couldn't hide its fiery nature. She had to be Jane, the oldest of the Willets' sisters.

The other young lady must have seen her start, for she turned to eye Caroline as well. Her hair was sleeker, her blue gaze surprisingly warm.

"Only Jenny has blue eyes." She heard Jeremy in her head, at least, what she'd come to think of as Jeremy's voice from his letters. "No one is sure how that happened, as the rest of us have either brown, gray, or green eyes."

"Can we help you?" Jenny asked.
Caroline lugged the valise closer. "I hope so. I was told this is the Willets' ranch."

A third girl came skipping around the house just then, only to pull up short, her copper-colored curls bouncing to a stop. "No, it's not," she said as if she had heard Caroline.

Caroline's stomach shriveled.

"Joy," Jane said in a warning.

"It isn't," she insisted, glancing at her two sisters. "Jack said I could name it. I decided on the Jumping J."

Caroline couldn't help her grin. "Because you all have names starting with J! Perfect!"

Now they all stared at her.

"Who are you?" Jane asked, putting herself in front of the others as if to protect them.

Oh, could she have introduced herself any worse? She stuck out her free hand. "Miss Caroline Cadhill. Your brother Jeremy likely mentioned me."

The three exchanged glances, and her hand fell with her hopes. Surely he'd talked about his courtship with his family. Had something happened to him since she'd received his last letter a month ago? Perhaps they'd written to her in Cincinnati, not knowing she was heading their way.

The front door of the house opened, and an older woman with warm brown hair came out onto the porch. About to shake a rag, she paused.

"Girls! You never told me we had company!"

His mother. It had to be. Caroline smiled at her, praying for recognition, acceptance.

"This is Miss Caroline Cadhill, Ma," Jane said, never taking her gaze off Caroline. "She says she's acquainted with Jeremy."

"Well, friends and acquaintances are always welcome," his mother replied. She tucked the rag into the pocket of her apron and motioned to Caroline. "Come on in now. Jane, see about refreshments. Jenny, fetch your Pa. Joy, go find your brother."

As if long used to being directed, the three sisters headed off in different directions.

Still not sure of her welcome, Caroline climbed the steps onto the porch and followed Mrs. Willets into the house. A hallway stretched from front to back alongside a staircase leading up. The room at the right appeared to be the dining room, with a large table and more chairs than she could count at a quick look. The walls were whitewashed, but the strawberry gingham curtains were bright and cheerful.

"How do you know my Jeremy?" his mother asked as she led her into the parlor on the left and took a seat on the horsehair sofa by the stone hearth.

Caroline set down her valise and put on her biggest smile. "I'm his mail-order bride."

Mrs. Willets blinked, then shook her head. "That boy. Is this another of his pranks?"

Pranks? *No, please, Lord, no!*

"I don't think so," Caroline managed. She nearly collapsed onto the nearest ladder-back chair. "He's been writing to me for months."

Somewhere, a door slammed, and footsteps thudded closer. A minute more, and a man stood framed in the doorway. He was tall, with the breadth of shoulders and length of legs the girls in Cincinnati would have mooned over. His hair was thick and as deep a red as the cattle he tended, and his green eyes caught the light from the window like the emerald ring that had been her mother's. The smile he directed at Caroline could only be called charming. Why, he was nearly as handsome as the view. Was her luck turning at last?

"You wanted me, Ma?" he asked in a voice that sounded very much like the one in her head.

"Jeremy," his mother said sternly. "I have just been introduced to your mail-order bride. What have you done?"

Jeremy Willets gaped at the woman who had appeared in the parlor like a bolt out of the blue. Caroline Cadhill was supposed to be in Cincinnati, more than two thousand miles away. Yet he couldn't deny that she looked much as she'd described herself in her letters.

"I'm not too tall," she'd written in one of their early correspondences. "My brother, Ned, is about six foot, and the top of my head comes just under his nose. He complains there's not enough meat on my bones, but I find it sufficient to keep me strong. At least, I've never been mistaken for a boy. My hair is the color of coal, and it has a few curls in it naturally. My eyes are brown."

Brown and big and staring back as if he were her last hope.

"Caroline?" he asked.

A smile blossomed, transforming her narrow face and

tugging at something inside him. "I *knew* you couldn't be teasing. Yes, it's me. I came to find you."

The scowl on his mother's face was sharp enough to nip the bud of delight at meeting Caroline at last. That reaction was precisely why he hadn't sent for Caroline yet. He and his family didn't always see eye to eye, and never more so than in the matter of love and marriage. Ma and Pa had taught them all to believe in, nay, extoll, the virtues of true love.

He had never been able to convince them that not everyone was cut out to find such a love, especially in a territory where men outnumbered women eight to one.

But none of that was Caroline's fault. She had come a far piece and on her own funding. A young lady alone. She had spunk, but he'd never doubted that, not after her letters.

He stepped into the room. "Well, how nice to finally meet you face to face."

"Yes," Ma put in before Caroline could respond. "It would have been nice if we had had any idea she was coming."

He loved his mother. Truly. But she was a force of nature. Best to calm the storm before it grew any larger.

Before he could smooth things over, however, Caroline jumped in.

"I'm truly sorry about that, Mrs. Willets," she said, smile contrite. "Things took a turn for the worse back home, and the only thing I could think of was to head West. Two trains, a steamer, and a couple of wagon rides later, and here I am."

Her smile was so pleased that even his mother thawed. "Well, you have traveled far. Why don't you rest a spell? I'll just help Jane with those refreshments." She rose and affixed him with a glare. "Jeremy, I'll need your assistance as well."

"Right behind you," Jeremy promised as she swept past

him into the hall. He darted to Caroline's side. "Proud of
you for getting here all on your own. That took courage.
Sorry if the welcome didn't live up to expectations. We
can be a cantankerous bunch."

She angled her head as if to spy his mother out the
door. "I hope I didn't get you into trouble."

"No more than usual," he assured her.

"Jeremy Dalton Willets!"

He grimaced. Just what every man wanted. To be
scolded by his mother in front of the woman he intended
to wed. With an apologetic look to Caroline, he strode
out the door.

His mother was waiting only far enough from the
parlor door that they might not be overheard. "A mail-
order bride!" she sputtered. "What were you thinking?"

"I was thinking that a man who's reached nine and
twenty years of age ought to be able to manage his own
courtship," he said, keeping his tone light and smile
endearing.

His mother drew in a breath. "I had hoped so as well.
Fine. Go talk to your bride then. We'll be along shortly."
She headed for the end of the corridor and the door to
the kitchen.

Shoulders feeling unaccountably tight in his flannel
work shirt, Jeremy returned to the parlor. Caroline was
perched on the edge of the chair, as if expecting to have
to flee any moment. Or maybe she thought his mother
would yank the chair out from under her.

He went to take the seat closest to hers. "I'm glad you
came."

Her eyes widened. He knew brown could be a rather
drab color, but her eyes swirled with green and gold as
well. In fact, he had a hard time pulling his gaze away.

"You are?" she asked.

"Yes, despite the welcome or lack thereof you received

from my family," he assured her. "I'm only sorry you felt the need to come all this way with no help."

She shrugged, the movement raising the loose gray wool coat that covered much of her plain blue dress. His sisters begged for any flounce or bit of lace. She didn't seem to have any.

"It was fine," she said. "You wouldn't believe all the sights you can see. At night, the whole sky lights up with stars!"

He nearly winced at the idea that she'd had to sit up all night, but he couldn't help but admire her ability to look on the bright side. That was one of the things he'd liked about her letters.

"I would have been happy to pay for a first-class ticket so you could have had a berth," he said. "And I could have met you in Olympia or Puget City."

She peered up at him shyly, thick black lashes fluttering. "That would have been nice. But I didn't want to put you to any trouble."

He glanced out the door. "Oh, I think I can get into trouble well enough on my own, but thanks."

He looked back at her to find her grimacing.

"I'm sorry," she murmured. "I thought they'd know about me."

They would have known if he'd have screwed his courage to the sticking point and told them. But he'd thought he had plenty of time. He and Caroline were only corresponding. No one had proposed or accepted yet. He could ease the idea into conversation with his family, prepare them for a bride they didn't know.

A marriage built more on companionship to start than love.

She kept gazing at him, eyes moving from his hair to his chin to his clothes. At least he'd shaved that morning. Sometimes after a night in the saddle, he didn't bother. A shame he hadn't dressed in his church clothes, but he'd hardly been expecting to meet his bride. At least the flannel shirt and twill trousers were practical and fairly clean.

But the more she looked, as if studying his very soul, the more he felt like squirming.

Not her too, Lord. Are You the only one who can appreciate me for who I am?

He found himself leaning back in the chair as if to escape the scrutiny and forced himself to relax. "I probably should have told them sooner," he admitted, "but I wasn't sure we'd decided we'd suit."

It was only the truth. Still, she might have taken umbrage. If she'd been willing to travel so far, she must have been far more sure than he had been.

She merely nodded. "I know. We hadn't made that decision yet. And I'm sorry to arrive all of a sudden like this. But I was in trouble, and I didn't know where else to turn."

Jeremy stiffened. "Trouble? What kind of trouble?"

She visibly swallowed. "The worst kind of trouble. Men came to the lodging house, threatening to hurt me if I didn't tell them where my brother had gone. I don't know where Ned is. He ran away a month ago, after Father was put in prison. I've been trying to manage on my own, but I just didn't feel safe anymore. Please, Jeremy, can I count on you to protect me?"

He could feel her fear, her worry. Something warned him he ought to feel as worried for his family. Had he brought trouble to their door?

But all he wanted to do was pull her close, comfort her.

A shame they were about to have an audience.

He contented himself with pressing his hand over hers as it lay on her skirts.

"You're safe here, Caroline," he promised. "You can stay for as long as need be."

Even if he had to battle his entire family to keep that promise.

Learn more at:
http://www.reginascott.com/suddenmob.html

OTHER BOOKS BY REGINA SCOTT

FORTUNE'S BRIDES SERIES
Never Doubt a Duke
Never Borrow a Baronet
Never Envy an Earl
Never Vie for a Viscount
Never Kneel to a Knight
Never Marry a Marquess
Always Kiss at Christmas
Never Pursue a Prince
Never Court a Count
Never Romance a Rogue
Never Love a Lord
Never Beguile a Bodyguard
Never Admire an Adventurer
Never Hire a Hero

GRACE-BY-THE-SEA SERIES
The Matchmaker's Rogue
The Heiress's Convenient Husband
The Artist's Healer
The Governess's Earl
The Lady's Second-Chance Suitor
The Siren's Captain

UNCOMMON COURTSHIPS SERIES
The Unflappable Miss Fairchild
The Incomparable Miss Compton
The Irredeemable Miss Renfield

The Unwilling Miss Watkin
An Uncommon Christmas

LADY EMILY CAPERS
Secrets and Sensibilities
Art and Artifice
Ballrooms and Blackmail
Eloquence and Espionage
Love and Larceny

MARVELOUS MUNROES SERIES
My True Love Gave to Me
The Rogue Next Door
The Marquis' Kiss
A Match for Mother

SPY MATCHMAKER SERIES
The Husband Mission
The June Bride Conspiracy
The Heiress Objective

THE REGENT'S DEVICES TRILOGY
(writing as R.E. Scott with Shelley Adina)
The Emperor's Aeronaut
The Prince's Pilot
The Lady's Triumph
The Aeronaut's Heart

FRONTIER MATCHES
The Perfect Mail-Order Bride
Her Frontier Sweethearts
Frontier Cinderella

And other books from Harper Collins, Mirror Press,
and Revell.

About the Author

REGINA SCOTT STARTED writing novels in the third grade. Thankfully for literature as we know it, she didn't sell her first novel until she learned a bit more about writing. Since her first book was published, her stories have traveled the globe, with translations in many languages including Dutch, German, Italian, and Portuguese. She now has more than 65 published works of warm, witty romance, and more than one million copies of her books are in reader hands.

While she adores the elegance of the Regency period in England and has penned many stories set then, she loves getting to write about history closer to her home in the Puget Sound area of Washington State, where she lives with her husband. She also loves diving into history headfirst. She has dressed as a Regency dandy, driven four-in-hand, learned to fence, and sailed on a tall ship, all in the name of research, of course. Learn more about her at *www.reginascott.com*.

www.ingramcontent.com/pod-product-compliance
Lightning Source LLC
Chambersburg PA
CBHW060447300726
48975CB00008B/2423